George Hatton Colomb

Donnington Castle

A royalist Story

George Hatton Colomb

Donnington Castle
A royalist Story

ISBN/EAN: 9783337082338

Printed in Europe, USA, Canada, Australia, Japan

Cover: Foto ©Andreas Hilbeck / pixelio.de

More available books at **www.hansebooks.com**

DONNINGTON CASTLE:

A ROYALIST STORY.

IN FOURTEEN STAVES.

WITH NOTES.

BY

COLONEL COLOMB,

Author of

'HEARTHS AND WATCHFIRES' and 'THE SHADOWS OF DESTINY.'

LONDON:

LONGMANS, GREEN, AND CO.

1871.

INTRODUCTORY.

*Letter to some person unknown concerning the poem
'Donnington Castle' and another work.*

At ye Signe of ye Blew Boare in Ivy Lane,
Oct. 23^d 1670.

Sir I dewly rec^d ye Bokes & hastene to in-
forme you th^t ye Poem shall be printed in the
newest & beste manner either in two or in one
Volume Q^{to}, another pocket edition (with gilte
leves) in twelves presentlie followinge. But Sir
y^r tearmes under favour are high, and I pray
you to remember how bad things be in ye Cittie
(God knoweth when they shall mende). Further-
more I beg leave to tell you th^t ye s^d poem
sholde doubtlesse abate somewhat of its valew
if it be not proven ye genuine handiwerke of
Colonel Richard[1] *Lovelace.* I pray you, therefore, let *Master Posthumous* furnish me spedilie,
not only with wh^t proofes there be that "*it was*
"*spoken by the Poet himself at a greate convivial*

Forsoothe
he shall
not fur-
nishe
them.

[1] The celebrated Kentish poet.

'Tis no suche greate matter whether he dyd or no.

"*Meeting in Kent ye laste Time ye Kentish men* "*rose,*" but also somewhat to shew that "*Sir* "*John Bois dyd comende ye Style and Matter,*" as you do affirme.

For w^h Proposition I crave you will excuse ye libertie ; for indeede S^r I do not in ye leaste question ye truthe of anie-thing you affirme, but I would observe that bothe ye worthy Gents. in question are now dead.

But it is neverthelesse true that *Master Starkey* of *Flete S^t* (wth whom I take it you are not unacquainted) saith, "that he hath had this "verie coppie of the Poem in hys owne hande, "and that it was brought to him by *Sir W^m* "*Davenant* long ago, who also said it was by "another hand, but th^t *Master Starkey* does in-"deed believe it to be *Sir Wm Davenant's* owne "writeing, and th^t ye Love p^ts were writ when "*S^r W^m* dyd strive with *Master May* for to be "Poet Laureate, w^h was long before ye late "Troubles dyd begin (w^h may very plainly be "seen by the alteracions)." All thys considered, 'tis but reasonable, Sir, by y^r leave, that you should abate somewhat. But, Sir, I should not be backwarde to offer you all ye sum you name, if the other[1] Boke by Will Lendall, Esq., about

Says Star-key so? Then he lyes.

I will not abate one Jotte.

---

[1] This MS. has also been preserved.

the great risynge in *Kent* in behalfe of His late
Maj^y be given to me to bring forth as a Venture
at ye same time.

Sir, I deal not at all in Musick, and though
ye song may, as you affirme, have been often-
times sunge at *the Globe* in Kinge *James's* tyme,
I do thinke the Poem might be more agreeablie
prefaced to the *Duke of Bucks.* than to the La.
you mention, seeing that *John Packer*, whose
house [1] *Denington Castle* was, was secretary to
ye said Duke's father. (*Master Phil. Packer*,[2]
hys son beinge also a verie gracious and ingenious gent.) Expectynge y^r pleasure,

I rest, y^{rs} hartilie,

ANDREWE PATERSON.

[margin: Tell him no. I owe nawt to ye Duke.]

P.S.—Sir, if the *Earle of Clarendon* be
writinge an History of the late Troubles, wee
in Cittie heare nothing thereof. I understand
not from youre Letter wheth^r this or some other
be the coppie w^h *Sir John Bois* dyd as you
say presente to ye Earle ye time he wente [3] over
in y^e *Nonsuche* to his presente Most Gracious
Maj^y wth tidyngs that ye Rumpe had founde its
Ende ?

[margin: Merke how he talketh of ye Rumpe, when 'tis well known he was a creature of Warner, Fowke, Gibbs, and Atkins of ye breeches !]

[1] See notes to Stave XII.
[2] For mention of this gentleman see *Evelyn's Sylva*, p. 166.
[3] See Diary of Pepys.

DONNINGTON CASTLE.

———+———

SONG DEDICATORY.

𝕮𝖔 𝕾𝖞𝖑𝖛𝖎𝖆.

FORASMUCHE as it is knowne that *Will Shakespeare* did oft-times and continuallie falle veric deep in Love, I holde th[t] my SYLVIA will not thinke it amisse if I here preface this my Historie of that faithfulle Knt. *Sir John Boys* wth a Dedication to Her, who descrveth beste y[e] Appelacion of "moste kinde" as well as of "moste fayre." That sadde Roundheade, but worthy Poet, *John Milton*, when he pay'd that jealous complimente to hys mightie Progenitor, saying, forsooth! that he but "warbled wyld native woodnotes," knew verie well that *Will* was much more than a Ballad-monger. All who do hold him lesse, shall be pleased to caste theyre eyes over the musicke followinge and claim, if they dare, y[e] authorshippe of y[e] Tune to which y[e] undoubted wordes are sett.

To Sylvia.

Ye
VIRGINALS.

Song.

Ye
VOICE.

1. Who is Sil - uia? what is she? That all our swaines com - mend
2. Is she kinde as she is faire? For beau - ty liues with kind -

her? Ho - ly, faire, and wise is she, The Heau'n such grace did lend her,
nesse! Loue doth to her eyes re-paire, To help him of his blind-nesse, And

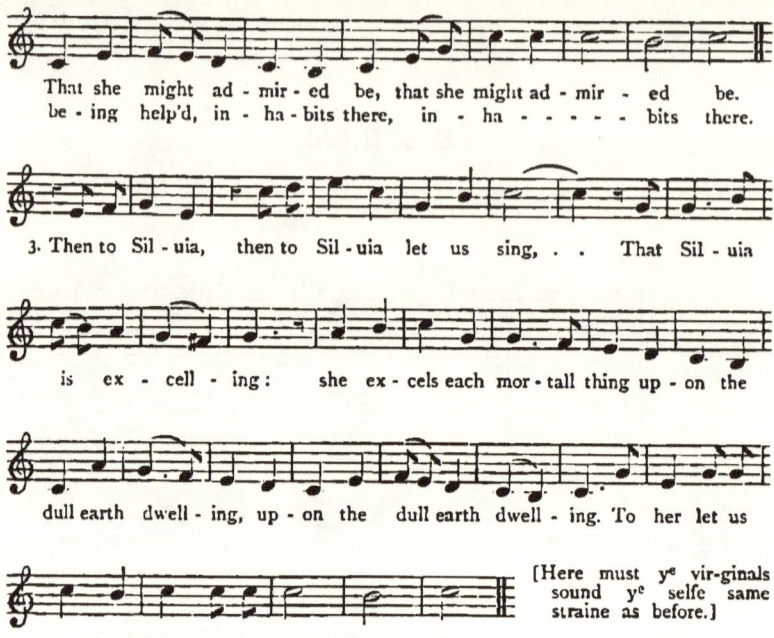

That she might ad - mir - ed   be, that she might ad - mir - ed   be.
be - ing help'd, in - ha - bits there, in - ha - - - - - bits   there.

3. Then to Sil - uia,   then to Sil - uia let us   sing, . .   That Sil - uia

is   ex - cell - ing: she ex - cels each mor - tall thing up - on the

dull earth dwell - ing, up - on the   dull earth dwell - ing. To her let us

[Here must yᵉ vir-ginals
sound yᵉ selfe same
straine as before.]

gar - lands bring, let us gar - - lands   bring!

CONTENTS.

STAVE   PAGE

   I. CASTLE AND CAVALIER 1

  II. OF BOYS AND THE BELOVED ELIZABETH 11

 III. OF BOYS AND THE MAID IN GREEN 23

 IV. THE FEAST . . . 37

  V. THE SONG 59

 VI. THE DANCE . 71

 VII. TO CHURCH . 83

VIII. THE RIVAL SHALL WIN 87

 IX. THE LOVE-KNOT TORN . . 103

  X. THE LOVE-KNOT TIED . . . 111

 XI. OF THE FORMER DAYS 121

 XII. THE SIEGE OF DONNINGTON 127

XIII. THE LAST ASSAULT 149

XIV. CASTLE AND CAVALIER TRIUMPHANT 177

DONNINGTON CASTLE :

A ROYALIST STORY.

———◆———

STAVE THE FIRST.

Castle and Cavalier.

B

DONNINGTON CASTLE:

A ROYALIST STORY.

*Supposed to have been narrated by the poet, in person, at a great
convivial meeting, in Kent, at the time the Kentish-men rose for
the King, in 1648.*

STAVE THE FIRST.

Castle and Cavalier.

I

The Royal Standard, proud and gay,
  O'er ruined[1] wall and rampart flies;
The watchful Castle stands at bay,
  And covenanting might defies;
To bar the London road it stands,
  With culverin all pointing down,
Lest arm'd rebellion's venturous bands
  Should reach the King at Oxford[2] town.

---

[1] The castle at the period the poet speaks of (Oct. 1644) had
already been several times battered and bombarded by the Parliament forces.

[2] Oxford was the seat of the King's Government from 1642 to
1646.

II

Dragooner[1] and musqueteer
From Newbury forth are gone,
In scarf[2] and with bandolier;[3]
The sun on their helmets shone:
With partizan, pike and spear,
The Parliament men came on!
     A victory there
       Hoping to gain,
     With a psalm and a prayer,
       And a battering[4] train;
For they thought to lay Donnington low as the ground;
     And, like Jericho's wall,
     That the Castle would fall
At the Puritan trumpet's sound!

III

But nought could those within appal,
    So stout and bold was each defender;
Colonel Boys, and his merry men all,
    Swore they would sooner die than surrender!

IV

Ladies and gallants, come list while I sing,
How Donnington Castle held out for the King!

[1] So termed in the King's *Articles of War*, Oxford, 1643. The dragoon, or dragooner, was an infantry soldier on horseback.

[2] Scarfs were worn by both parties, sometimes over the shoulder and sometimes round the waist, the colour being the distinguishing badge.

[3] Bandolier contained charges of powder.

[4] Siege artillery.

V

But I hold it wise to warn you, before
I begin—that if here there be Covenant men,
They will carp at a story of love and war,
Set down by a Royalist pen.
But to show you how deeply I value their snarls,
Here goes my hat[1] to the roof for King Charles.

VI

The Cavalier for Royal cause
Will toil endure, and danger brave ;
But while he fights for King and laws,
A mistress true he still must have.
Did Colonel Boys of faithful love
Next to his heart no token wear—
Portrait in little,[2] flow'r, or glove,
The cherished gift of lady fair ?

VII

Would you learn at what shrine he did kneel or fall,
The upward course you must with me trace
Of the stream of time that floweth apace,
And events of a former day recall.

[1] This appears to have been the frequent signal for reaction in
favour of the King after the loyal party had been suppressed. For
example, when the Surrey petitioners thronged into Westminster
Hall, May 16, 1648, a *Diurnal* of that period relates that ‘ the
club-men of Surrey,’ raising ‘ a combustion’ in the Hall, ‘ pressing
upon the court of guard, threw up their hats for King Charles.’—See
King's Pamphlets, 1648.
[2] Miniature.

Leave we, then, him and his merry men all,
    As to their posts on the ramparts they go,
    Running with bullet[1] and match[2] to and fro,
    Or pointing the minion[3] and culverin[4] low—
        Making all ready to meet the foe,
        With bang[5] for bang, and with blow for blow,
    While loud rings the trumpet on Donnington wall.

VIII

Now Berkshire fades upon the sight,
To southern fields we take our flight,
Washed by the Thames and by the sea,
' Unconquered '[6] boasting still to be.

IX

Ye men of Kent, and Kentish men,
    What though full oft the poet's hand
Hath touched with glorifying pen
    The praises of your favoured land ;

---

[1] Now called round shot.   [2] Slow and quick match.

	Bore	Weight	Wght. of shot	Chge.	Point blank range	Extreme range
	inches	lbs.	lbs.	lbs.	paces	paces
[3] Minion (a piece of ordnance . .	3½	1,000	4	4	150	1,500
[4] Culverin (a piece of ordnance) .	5½	4,500	17½	12	200	2,500

                        —See *Monson's Tracts*, p. 342.

[5] ' Scotch Montrose hath lately well *banged* the rebels.'—*News-letter. Report of Royal Commission on Hist. MSS.*, 1870.

    ' 'Tis well known that black Tom Fairfax ' (Lord Fairfax) ' and his tatter-rags ' (the Parliament army) ' got a *bang* from the Kentish men.'—*Tract printed in* 1648, *King's Pamphlets.*

[6] ' Invicta ' is the motto of Kent.

To touch them lightly once again,
　　Can I refuse at your command?
No; for the minstrel's heart must yield
To Beauty's charm, by truth revealed.

X

From all her sister shires so gay,
Sweet Kent doth bear the palm away;
For England makes her garden there:
Her swains are brave, her maids are fair;
Flow'rs, stars, and eyes do brightly shine,
Where climbing hops with roses twine,
Where cherry orchards bloom in spring,
And nightingales in chorus sing.
'INVICTA' be thy motto still!
　　May hostile envy plot in vain
Thy fields to spoil, thy sons to kill,
　　Thy hearths and altars to profane!
May the white cliffs that skirt the sea,
A wall impregnable still be
To Kent the fair and Kent the free![1]

XI

Have you heard of the Conqueror's Roll of fame,
　　Recording the names of his followers all,
Who under his banner from Normandy came?
　　Suspended it was upon Battle[2] wall:

---

[1] It is almost superfluous to remark that both 'men of Kent' and 'Kentish-men' to this day boast that 'they have never been conquered.'

[2] The Battle Abbey Roll.

Among the names which were writ thereon,
The Herald will tell you that Boys was one.
If further you question, he'll answer again :
' In Kent his descendants have flourished since then.'
But I come not pedigree here to prove,
But to sing you a story of war and of love,
                    ' Boys of Bonnington '—
    This is the title the Herehaughte[1] saith
Of the Colonel[2] brave whom we left at Donnington,
    Royalist true to the death !
The scene we shift, and we shift the time,
For both are commanded in minstrel's rhyme.

                    XII

        In the jovial days of old,
            Ere treason had begun
        Its projects fierce and bold,
            In sixteen-forty-one.[3]

---

[1] Herald.

[2] ' Bonnington is an ancient seat near Godneston, from whence the numerous families of the Bois took their origin; and from hence was branched out into those divisions of their names who have settled at Fredville, Betshanger, Hawkhurst, and other places in this county; and they all derive themselves from John de Bosco, who is mentioned in the Roll of Battle Abbey among such gentlemen as came into England with William I.; and at this place they had inhabited for seventeen descents in Phillipot's time, when Bonnington was in possession of that brave soldier Sir John Boys, to whose coat armour King Charles I. gave the augmentation of a crown imperial or, on a canton azure, for his service at Donnington Castle, Berkshire.' —*Harris's Hist. of Kent.* See also *Hasted's Hist. of Kent,* ix. 245, 6. For the pedigree of Boys see *Berry's County Genealogies ;* ' Kent.'

[3] The year of Strafford's execution, Laud's impeachment, the Irish massacre, and the Grand Remonstrance.

How gaily passed the time !
   We did both dance and sing,
And 'twas not made a crime
   If we did pledge ' the King.'
The laws we did uphold ;
   The Church was honour'd then ;
And we were only bold
   'Gainst foes of Englishmen.
Now mirth and joy are dead,
   And gloom is over all ;
For freedom also fled
   When Charles did leave Whitehall.[1]
The Church—the laws—are gone !
   And Englishmen do learn,
Against themselves alone
   Their deadly blows to turn !

XIII

The former days, the former days !
   Which all too lightly we did prize—[2]

[1] The Civil War commenced virtually on the retirement of the King from Whitehall (to Hampton Court, and finally to York), after the failure of his attempt to seize Kimbolton and the five members. Soon afterwards the Parliament seized the power of the Militia, and issued their Commission of Array.

[2] 'During the whole time . . which was a period of above twelve years (1628 to 1640) this kingdom . . enjoyed the greatest calm and the fullest measure of felicity that any people in any age for so long a time have been blessed with, to the wonder and envy of all other parts of Christendom. . . But all these blessings could but enable—could not compel us to be happy.'—

Oh ! could we bring them back again,
With playmates lost and brothers slain !
Alas ! the thought is vain, is vain,
    And tears do mount into mine eyes !

XIV

Pledge we the cup, but in silence all,
To the days and the friends we can never recall !

Clarendon's Hist. of the Rebellion, vol. i. p. 131. Oxford, 1826.
Elsewhere Clarendon uses the expression 'those jolly days,' in allu-
sion to the same period.

STAVE THE SECOND.

Of Boys and the beloved Elizabeth.

STAVE THE SECOND.

Of Boys and the beloved Elizabeth.

I

The Weald of Kent was mantled with snow,
  And the wind piped shrill through the oak-woods hoar;
    For sharp was the season of Christmas-tide
In sixteen hundred and thirty four.
    Rivers to summer level had dried
With white ice checking the current's flow;
  Hard and black was the ice on the mere;
  Starry the sky; and, her crescent clear
  (As it were crystal with silver combining),
    Royal Diana did coldly show,
  With golden Venus beside her shining!
Decked with green was the old church quire,
      Where the Vicar his evensong saw has said,
      With blessing for living, and hope for the dead.
    Decked with green were both chamber and hall,
Where the ynle-log hissed on the sea-coal fire;
    Young and old, rich and poor, wise and foolish, and all,
    Assembled at hospitality's call,
    Awakened the echoes of roof and wall
Which music and mirth inspire.

II

' No, not a note of the carol I'll play ! '
The lovely Elizabeth [1] said ;
   ' Here I sit dumb,
   Until Boys be come,
  Though it be until New Year's day ! '
And the youths and the maids of the chorus she led
 Saw she must have her way ;
For the crotchet she once took into her head,
 She would keep spite of animadversions,
   With perverseness strange,
   And defiant of change
As the laws of the Medes and Persians.
To what beauty decrees all subservient must be,
And fairest of fair Kentish maidens was she.

III

 Would I could paint you her charms so rare !
  Oh, if Sir Anthony Vandyck had been
That evening within her with-drawing-room there
Soon would his pencil, the vision recalling,
  Have drawn you a portrait [2] passing fair
   Of this sweet uncrownèd Queen.

---

[1] Elizabeth Fotherby, daughter of Sir John Fotherby, of Barham Court, Kent.—See *Berry's County Genealogies ;* 'Kent.'

[2] I cannot find any portrait of this lady, but the *Sutherland Catalogue* mentions more than one of 'John Boys.' The Rev. Thos. Boys, M.A., grandson of the historian of Sandwich, and a descendant of Vincent Boys, possesses one in oils, painted probably at the Restoration. It is not a very good painting, but it is no doubt genuine.

Her form enchanting, her sprightly air,
Her beautiful face, and her dark brown hair
Over her shoulders so gracefully falling;
A nose that not Phidias' art could improve,
And lips that seemed melting with pity and love;
But how would the art of the master surprise
Could he fix but one flash of those exquisite eyes!

IV

And the lovely Elizabeth neither would sing,
   Nor a note of the virginals touch or sound,
Though the youths and the merry maids, all in a ring,
   With their parts from the score there were gather'd
      around.
Treble, contralto, tenor, and base
Bore disappointment with passable grace;
Though some of the gallants in doublets gay,
   And in silken hose, with the riband[1] rosette
   On their new buff shoes so daintily set,
Seemed not at all to approve the delay;
      And one of the fair,
      Whisper'd jestingly there:
' Lawyers the contract make ready to sign;
   ' Worthless the parchment if irksome the vow—
· Poor Sir Nathaniel his prize may resign,
   ' Master John Boys is the favourite now.
' When Sir Nathaniel[2] from Spain shall return,
   ' How it will please him, such tidings to learn!'

---

[1] In fashion during the whole of the Caroline period. Buckles, however, came in early in Charles II.'s reign.

[2] Sir Nathaniel Finch (supposed to have been about this time, or

Then the lovely Elizabeth rose from her chair,
　　And went to the oriel narrow and high,
And, lifting the hangings embroider'd fair,
　　Looked out on the snow and the frosty sky,
And the moonlight dim on the oak-woods hoar;
　　　　And then did declare
　　　　To the company there,
She had never known Boys to be late before.

　　　　　　　　v

But he came not yet, though the evening waned,
Though crescent Diana the zenith had gain'd,
Though the feast was laid, though the hall did fill,
Master John Boys—he was absent still;
And mute were virginals, voice, and tongue,
　　And silent the score[1] on the instrument lay;
This is the carol that should have been sung,
　　If *primo tenore* had not been away—
Of the words I do make you free ;
　　But first I must tell you that if there be here
Any king-cozening, kingdom-destroying, church-over-
　　turning, schismatical knave,[2]
　　Who only fasts and long faces would have—

earlier, betrothed to Sir John Fotherby's daughter).—*Berry's County
Genealogies*; 'Kent.'

[1] Part-singing was very common up to this period. In the reign
of Charles II. solo singing was more in vogue.

[2] This language, though breathing somewhat of the party spirit
of the period, is much milder than that commonly used. The
Roundheads were sometimes smart in their retorts, calling the Cavaliers 'lamentable tag-rags,' 'highflying d—m—e ranters,' 'cur
spaniels,' 'drinkers of hellish healths to their own damnation,'
&c. &c.

Any who frowns upon Christmas glee,
Any who thinks that his garland green[1]
Only borrow'd from pagan has been ;
  Or who Beelzebub fancies he spies
When blazes burn blue on nativity[2] pies ;
Or who'd give to all masquers short shrift and a rope—
  Or, Anti-Christ's ending,
  Would compass by sending
All mortal plum-puddings down throat of the Pope—
To such I would say—Stick your thumbs in your
  ears ;
    To murder the king
    Is a very small thing,
And grind to the dust all the poor Cavaliers ;
But lost is the sinner who roundelay hears !

----

[1] A Puritan writer of this period says: ' Sacred rites were done
unto Saturn (because he found out the grafting of trees), and the
25th of December, with the rest of the days following (seven days
together) were appointed and generally observed by the idolatrous
heathen. To that end sacrifices, sports, and other solemnities, were
magnificently and with great rejoicing prepared, which the apostle
tells us is sacrificing to Divils. . . May Day was consecrated and
kept in honour of their Divil Goddesse Flora, a notable rich ——,
at what time they used to bring laurel, green boughs, branches of
trees, and flowers, with singing and rejoicing, to adorn their doors.
The 1st of November was solemnly kept by the Pagans in honour of
all their Divil Deities. . . At Christmas the Divil is more served
than at any other time of the year.'

[2] Mince pies. The shapes in which they are moulded still retain
something of the cradle form.

Nor Marshal,[1] nor Dell,[2] nor Hugh Peters[3] will shrive
  ye
Who list to a carol called—

Holly and Ivy.

1

O'er dale and hill, and o'er waste and wold,
  Its chill white mantle doth winter fling;
Though December be dark and cold,
  Our fresh green garlands foretaste the spring.
See the berries so ruby bright,
  Peeping under the shining leaves,
Father Christmas his wreath to-night
  All of holly and ivy weaves.

Chorus.

Holly and ivy, holly and ivy,
  Frosts of winter that still defy;
Holly and ivy, holly and ivy,
  Holly and ivy—who'll buy, who'll buy?

[1] Stephen Marshal, an eminent Presbyterian minister, who, according to Walker, ratted to the Independents when he found them on the winning side, although he had a chief hand in compiling the *Directory.*

[2] Another great Puritan divine.

[3] The renowned Hugh Peters.

2

At your feet our treasures we pour,
  Slips and branches both short and tall;
Take your choice from the verdant store,
  Deck the chamber, the church, the hall!
Hospitality's ancient crown
  Royal brow of old Yule must shade;
All know, who at his shrine bow down,
  Of holly and ivy that crown is made.

Chorus.

Holly and ivy, holly and ivy,
  Haste and choose, for the time doth fly;
Holly and ivy, holly and ivy,
  Holly and ivy—who'll buy, who'll buy?

3

When sweet music with festive sound
  Moves to friendship and wakes to love,
While the loving-cup circles round,
  Our gay pennon must wave above;
Though the season hath icy fangs—
  Cold though bloweth the winter storm—
Where the holly and ivy hangs,
  Thoughts are kindly, and hearts are warm!

c 2

Chorus.

Holly and ivy, holly and ivy,
   With the garlands of spring may vie ;
Holly and ivy, holly and ivy,
   Holly and ivy—who'll buy, who'll buy?

4

If perchance in your hearts should rise
   Thoughts of joys that are past and o'er,
While lamenting with tearful eyes
   Some who come to the feast no more,
Still the holly and ivy twine !
   Weave the garland that laughs at gloom,
Love and friendship again shall shine
   Green and deathless beyond the tomb !

Chorus.

Holly and ivy, holly and ivy,
   Frosts of winter that still defy ;
Holly and ivy, holly and ivy,
   Holly and ivy—who'll buy, who'll buy ?

Holly and Ivy.

Ye VIRGINALS.

Allegretto.

rall.............

Carol.

Ye VOICE.

O'er dale and hill and o'er waste and wold, Its chill white mantle doth

win - ter fling; Tho' De-cem-ber be dark and cold, Our green garlands fore-

taste the Spring. See the ber-ries so ru - by bright, Peep-ing un-der the

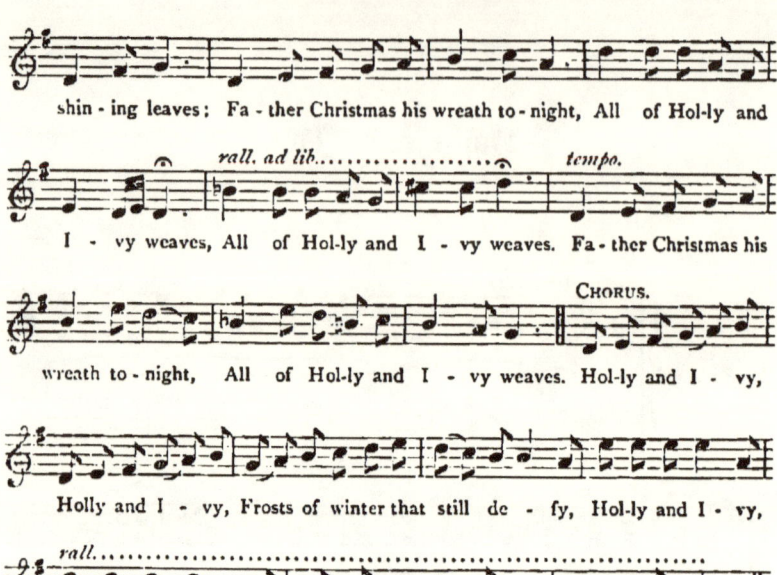

shin - ing leaves: Fa - ther Christmas his wreath to - night, All   of Hol-ly and

I - vy weaves, All   of Hol-ly and I - vy weaves. Fa - ther Christmas his

wreath to - night,   All   of Hol-ly and I - vy weaves. Hol-ly and I - vy,

Holly and I - vy, Frosts of winter that still de - fy, Hol-ly and I - vy,

Hol - ly and I - - vy,   Hol - ly and I - vy, Who'll buy? who'll buy?

STAVE THE THIRD.

Of Boys and the Maid in Green.

STAVE THE THIRD.

Of Boys and the Maid in Green.

I

And where was Boys?
Fitly the question the moment employs ;
And for an answer I hold it best
To lead you in search of the absent guest.

II

To answer the peerless Elizabeth's call
To join in the carol and feast in the hall,
The gallant that morning had mounted his steed ;
The snow-drifts were high, and the way it was long,
But where is the lover obstruction will heed ?
Beguiling the journey with snatches of song,
At times he did gallop—at times he did creep,
When downs they were open, or roads they were deep,
As over the Weald he came riding along;
And oft, as her face o'er his mem'ry came,
He murmur'd his darling enchantress's name.

III

From London his journey the gallant had made ;
Last night at the house of a kinsman he stayed.

IV

Boys was handsome, brave, and young,
　Stout and active too was he ;
If by men his praise was sung,
　For a bearing bold and free,
That he had a winning tongue,
　Ladies fair did all agree.
Honest heart and open hand
Love and friendship will command.
Ready still the poor to aid,
　And to gen'rous deeds inclined,
Seldom by self-int'rest sway'd,
　Slow to anger—courteous—kind—
Full of pity was his heart,
With the weaker taking part.
If depress'd by fortune's frown,
Not for long was he cast down,
For a spirit gay he had,
Banishing reflection sad.
Bright his smile, and loud his laugh,
　Smart he was at repartee,
Song could sing, and health could quaff,
　And excelled in mimicry ;
Skilled in manly exercises,
　He was (and description here
　Ends in phrase that all comprises)
An ' accomplished Cavalier.'

V

Arms his trade—he followed Mars—
And in the Low Country wars
Five years'[1] service he had done,
And had fame and credit won.

VI

He don'd his plumed hat and his cloak trimmed with furs,
    To visit his lady-love fair and confiding,
In laced velvet doublet, buff-boots and gilt spurs,
    Far over the Weald he came gallantly riding;
His locks o'er a Flemish-lace collar descended,
A fair broider'd baldric his rapier suspended;
His wallet behind, and good pistols before him,
And worthy the rider the charger that bore him.
Boys still to the eastward kept turning his eye
Where castle-enchanted far distant doth lie.

VII

Redly now the evening ray
Falls across his wintry way,
While he slackens speed again.
    Hazel-thicket crashing through
    Near the woods of Horsemonden,[2]

[1] See original letter of Colonel Boys in *Rupert Correspondence, Addl. MSS. Bh. Musm.*

[2] Another name appears to have been erased from the original MS.

Where a bridle-path he knew,
Arch'd by trees—where snow would fall
Scant and sparsely—if at all.

VIII

Hark! he hears a loud halloo,
  Down a dark sequester'd glade,
And he soon became aware
  That a voice did call for aid
In behalf of lady fair,
  By marauding knaves waylaid.

IX

In apparel all of green,
  (Of like colour was her hat)
With a mask upon her face,
  On a palfrey white she sat;
Small her form, but full of grace,
  And to fabled Fairy Queen,
Some resemblance you might trace.
      Golden brown
      Her hair hung down,
  Slender wand of silver sheen
  In her hand she bore;
By her side to guard her stood
One attired like Robin Hood.
Boys, when he had scann'd him o'er,
      Turn'd his eyes the fairy on,
      And he knew Maid Marion,
Mimic Queen of good Green-Wood.

Spite of all their fine array
Only Christmas masquers they!

X

This, which time to tell employs,
Yet was seen in briefest glancing,
While to rescue was advancing
    Master Boys.

XI

Well for that poor damsel fair,
  That a champion bold was near;
And for her companion there—
  Truly both had cause to fear;
Four well-arm'd and sturdy thieves,
  Gather'd round them, Boys perceives!

XII

Two with trenchant blades all bare
  Had engaged the man in green,
Quarterstaff who tried to wield
In a vain attempt to shield
  From a third the forest queen;
While a fourth with matchlock spanned
(Captain of the murd'rous band)
In the pathway took his stand,
Threat'ning, with blaspheming word,
Death—if man or palfrey stirred,
Or if cry for help was heard;
Levelling, while those words he said,
Matchlock at poor Robin's head.

XIII

Dead the old man had been laid,
  For he made resistance brave,
Had not Boys through thicket bounding
  Ridden down the hardy knave,
Who o'er Marion flourish'd blade,
Thus the leader's aid confounding
Who his comrade tried to aid.

XIV

  Boys and charger interpose
  'Twixt the masquers and their foes;
With one hand a pistol aiming
  Rapier in the other waves,
Anger in his aspect flaming,
  'Hence!' he cries, 'ye murd'ring knaves'
  (Loud and threat'ning was his tone)
  'Let the man and maid alone!'

XV

Ping! the ball hath missed him clean.
      Seized with fear
      The buccaneer [1]
Fires and flies through briar and bush;
Off his three companions rush;
Safety in retreat they find;

---

[1] Probably an ancestor of the smugglers who a century later infested these parts.

And as hare
Eludes the snare,
Scarce a trace they left behind.

XVI

Scarce a trace !
Alas ! alas !
Trace sufficient left there was,
Though so swift the robber's pace.

XVII

In the little palfrey's side
Ugly gash the thief had made,
For the ball the ribs had flayed
When at Boys he shot so wide !
Fierce the smart—
With sudden start,
Palfrey springs, and Marion falls—
But upon her feet she lands ;
Sight she sees that heart appals
While the pony quiet stands—
From the wound the crimson flow
Hotly welling,
Broadly swelling,
Drips and patters on the snow !

XVIII

' Oh !' she cries, and clasps her hands,
' Daisy's hurt—my darling Daisy—
' They have shot my Daisy dead,

' Curst the deed
    ' To make him bleed,
' Would that I had died instead !
' What possess'd me thus to roam
' With my pet so far from home ?
' Wherefore came I forth this way ?
' What his crime I do not know,
' That he should be punish'd so !
' Would I ne'er had seen this day !
' Out upon the cruel knave
' Who hath slain my palfrey brave ! '

XIX

Still, but trembling, Daisy stood,
    As the maid with kerchief white
Strove in vain to stanch the blood,
    Though she sicken'd at the sight ;
Closer to his side she crept,
    And with arm round neck and crest,
       Gently pressing,
    Tried to clasp him to her breast ;
    And, her wounded pet caressing,
Lifted up her voice and wept.

XX

' By St. George ! ' Boys mutter'd then,
    ' Could my hand yon villain reach,
    ' I would lesson to him teach
' He should ne'er forget again ;
' Sadder sight I ne'er shall know—

' 'Tis enough to mar one's sleeping—
' Little palfrey wounded so,
' Little maiden o'er him weeping !
 ' But although the fact be plain
 ' The conclusion may be vain—
 ' How could he have meant to shoot
 ' Dumb and inoffensive brute ?
 ' Or at maid direct a ball ?
 ' No, 'twas accidental all.'

XXI

Now he looks at Daisy's wound,
And though something deep 't was found—
Comfort to the maid he gives,
While he pats her on the shoulder :—
 ' Dry thine eyes ; thy palfrey lives ;
 ' Though his hurt be sad and sore,
' Ere he shall be two months older,
 ' Daisy you shall mount once more—
 ' See, already on the snow,
 ' Scantier falls the crimson flow.'

XXII

Said her comrade—' He speaks true.
' Sir, our thanks we owe to you,
' Who such deadly peril braved,
' And two strangers' lives have saved.
' Niece, to merit give its due,
' And our kind deliverer thank.'

* D

XXIII

But the little maiden shrank
  From what seemed too hard a task ;
  From behind impervious mask
She a friend had recognised,
  And her little tongue was tied,
  Though to speak to him she tried,
For the sight her heart surprised.
  She her uncle takes aside—
  ' Oh ! 'tis he !' at length she cried :
O'er her neck a crimson glow
  All at once began to flame !
Boys the cause had chanced to know
  Had he heard the damsel's name,
  Had he learnt from whence she came,
Had he then her features scanned,—
  But when masks conceal the face,
  Hard identity to trace,
As we all can understand.

XXIV

Though that changing hue he saw
No conclusion did he draw,
For the maiden, sooth to say,
O'er his thoughts had little sway ;
  Compass pointeth toward the north—
Steadily his flame is burning,
If in two directions turning
  What would gallant's love be worth ?

XXV

Much he longs to break away,
For the evening groweth late,
Feast in Barham Hall doth wait,
And Elizabeth the Fair,
Sweet enchantress, reigneth there !
But from claim of charity
How can errant knight be free ?
Low he mutters, ' Oh, if only
' I could leave this maiden here !
' But the wood is wide and lonely,
' And the thieves may still be near.
' Though disguised from curious gaze,
' Thus in masquerade they go,
' Gentle blood their talk betrays,
' And I cannot leave them so ;
' Old the uncle—yes, I see
' I must still their escort be ! '

XXVI

Kind assistance now he proffers,
And his steed the damsel offers,
To the palfrey saddle shifts,
Pillion on the charger lifts—
For by chance they let him know
That the self-same road they go.
Soon the maid o'er parting grieves ;
Daisy roadside inn receives ;
Sorry nag his load relieves.

D 2

XXVII

Neighbouring justice briefly told
Of the thieves who haunt the wold;
Forward go the three together,
Facing the inclement weather,
    For the north-east wind is cold;
Boys of feast and song despairing
Maiden's company is sharing,
    While the stars do light their way,
In a silence all unbroken
Not a word the maid has spoken,
    Boys had not a word to say;
For himself he is consoling
    That to-morrow—Christmas-day—
While the Christmas hymn is rolling
    Sweetly down the chancel fair,
    Kind Elizabeth shall there
(As her wont on Sundays is)
    Sit beside him,
With her soft white hand in his.

STAVE THE FOURTH.

The Feast.

STAVE THE FOURTH.

The Feast.

I

The hospitable board was spread,
A goodly company was there,
Of gallants brave and ladies fair,
And Christmas garlands overhead
From roof-tree arch suspended were ;
  With verdure sheen
  To grace the scene,
They sparkled in the misty air.
Before the cupboard decked with plate
A table on the dais stood,
Where kith and kin together sat
With knights and dames of highest blood.
  While down the hall
  Was room for all,
And entertainment choice and good
For rich and poor, and great and small,
  Who came to prove the dainty fare,
  And hospitable welcome there.

II

To feast the pipe and tabor call
And set the rafters ringing,
   From gallery of ancient hall
The choir-men loud are singing,
   While serving-men, so straight and tall,
The boar's head in are bringing.
Hark !—' *Caput apri defero!*'—on high the chorus rises—
With holly-sprigs and rosemary
The boar's head well must garnished be,
No Englishman, but Jew is he,
The boar's head who despises !

III

      Aunt Grace
      Kept a place
Next to where lovely Elizabeth sat ;
By her side was a chaplain fat,
And a conventicle-man was he,
Who did not care much for frivolity,
Though he liked the lovely Elizabeth's aunt
(Somebody said that he money did want).
' Niece Elizabeth,' said Aunt Grace,
' Remember, I have reserved this place.'
      But who it was for
         She would not tell,
      Though in her heart
         She knew very well.
(The sequel will show you I speak what is true).

'Aunt Grace,'
Elizabeth said,
'As for the place—
'I've reserved it too.'

IV

'*Too*—you?
'Pray who,
'Mistress Elizabeth, will you put there?'
'Aunt, for concealment I do not care,
'Though revelation perchance annoys,
'I have reserved it for Master Boys.'

V

Aunt Grace
Commanded her face—
Scarcely a sign of her thought could you trace—
Wreathed in smiles did her features appear,
But she said, 'Is it wise to ask him here?
'Surely you cherish a profitless flame,
'When Sir Nathaniel your hand must claim.
'Boys must be placed lower down in the hall,
'He cannot sit near us, whate'er may befall.'
But Elizabeth said, 'He shall.'

VI

Aunt Grace,
Proud of her race,
Made up the match with Nathaniel Finch,
And was determined her niece shouldn't flinch,

For Sir Nathaniel a title bore,
And he had money and lands good store ;
And at the court he could favour win,
As he was of the Lord Keeper's[1] kin.

VII

Aunt Grace,
With paint on her face,
Thought 'mongst the beauties of court to have place—
Her friends could remains of well-favouredness trace—
Once she had been to a masque at Whitehall,
And fairest of all
There reckon'd had been—
But at that time she was only sixteen.

VIII

Sir John and Mistress Elizabeth's mother
Loved not at all too much trouble and pother.

[1] Sir John Finch, afterwards Baron Finch of Fordwich. He had a house called the Mote, near Canterbury. He was one of the great supporters of Ship-money, and after Strafford and Laud had been impeached fled to Holland, and so escaped their fate. He is alluded to by ballad-writers of the period as follows, in connection with the unpopular Bishop Wren :—

'The little *Wren* that soars so high,
Thought on his wings away to fly,
Like *Finch*, I know not whither.'

And again :—

'Ask me no more why little Finch
From Parliament began to winch,
Since such as dare to hawk at kings
Can easily clip a *Finch's* wings.'—See *Rump Ballads.*

Aunt Grace
Ruled in their place,
Except when the lovely Elizabeth chose,
Who sometimes her counsels did hotly oppose,
Between them was open war;
But a purpose crossed,
Or a battle lost,
Aunt Grace very patiently bore.
For she had studied an old Scotch rhyme,
When she wanted to win, ' she could bide her time.'
But Elizabeth's mother and good Sir John
Looked with favour their[1] sister upon;
Once when Sir John was nearly undone,
And had the constable wholly outrun,
Aunt Grace
Mended his pace,
Helped him to jog on his way once more,
Bailiffs and creditors drove from the door,
Acres and manor-house back she won;
How she contrived it you'll gather anon.
Strange is the web of human affairs;
Some, who have nothing but selfish ends,
Lighten distresses and banish cares,
And are to their fellow-creatures friends.
Various the means by which Providence works,
Benefit often in evil things lurks.
Always Aunt Grace was a riddle to me;
Some, who are far more gentle of mood,
With better intentions do far less good.

---

[1] 'Sisters-in-law' were at this period commonly called 'sisters.'

Half Presbyterian she boasted to be—
I think she affected more liberty
    Than Archbishop Laud to a lady would give;
The Catechism she liked not all,
And did not much care for the hints of St. Paul,
    And without ornaments scarcely could live.
The woman for crotchet religious who fights,
    Against the devil still holds her own;
And though she be saint will stick out for her rights,
    And e'en with arch-angels won't lower her tone.
Enough for the present you've heard of Aunt Grace,
    Further description I now defer;
I pray you remember a vacant space
    Is left to-night 'twixt her niece and her!
Aunt Grace and Sir John's fair daughter
Were sympathetic as oil and water.

IX

    At Barham is the feast begun
      For hospitality renown'd,
    And on the festal tide doth run,
      And busy knives do clatter round;
    And all is jollity and fun,
      And merry laughter walls resound.
Good beef and venison grace the board,
And wine from flagons high is poured,
And home-brew'd ale that hath been stored
    Since daffodils[1] were blowing.

---

[1] 'March beer.'

Substantial cheer
And wine and beer,
Do set the spirits flowing.

X

The dais—oh ! the sight was fair
  Where gentles all are dining,
The courtly gallants dressed with care
  In lace and velvet shining,
The dames who silks and satins wear,
  With pearls[1] their locks entwining.
The sight to poor men pleasure gave—
The poor do love apparel brave.
Imagine not—thou envious knave—
  That daughters, wives, and mothers,
Because fine clothes they cannot have,
  In rags would see all others.

XI

But while the tide of joy doth flow,
  There's more 'mongst lads and lasses,
Who quaffing sit, the salt below,
  From cans instead of glasses,
For oft the joy that gentles know
  The vulgar joy surpasses.
Then long live ancient jollity !
To change old England's polity,

---

[1] Strings of pearls in the hair, as well as pearl necklaces, were common at this time.

I hold it but frivolity
    In politicians daring;
You only find equality
    Where all in mirth are sharing.

XII

Equality of joys may be,
But yet 'tis thing you rarely see;
In midst of mirth will sadness steal
Where all should equal pleasure feel.

XIII

Behold near yonder vacant space,
A shadow clouds the fairest face!
Wont to be gayest at the feast,
The loveliest there, had joy the least—
Of all, the envy and the pride,
She was the only one who sighed—
Hilarity was all forgot,
For this her thought—'He cometh not!'

XIV

Joy for Elizabeth there's none,
    Nor sign of joy there doth appear,
Although the feast speeds gaily on,
    And wine doth flow all hearts to cheer;
Both flesh and fowl from board are gone,
    Plum pottage and minch-pies[1] they clear.

---

[1] *Sic*, often in books of the Caroline period.

'He comes not yet!—He is not here!'
And when the loving-cup went round,
And music swelled to softer sound,
Her starry eyes with tears did fill,
For Master Boys was absent still!

XV

And one that ill his place supplied
His lovely fere [1] did sit beside.
Upon the right—the vacant space
Divides her from her foe, Aunt Grace—
A cousin filled the left-hand place.
There, Anthony to please her tried,
By letting forth a ceaseless flow
Of stories gossiping and low,
To which, though seeming ear she lent,
At one came in, at t'other went.

XVI

'Fair coz, wont to be free and gay,
'Why now so dull—be pleased to say.'
("Twas half in earnest, half in joke,
The talking Anthony here spoke.)
'Arouse thee, coz—from court of Spain
'Nathaniel Finch soon comes again!
'Divided it is sad to be,
'From those we love, by leagues of sea;

[1] Sweetheart.

‘ And monthly billets scarcely prove
‘ Sufficient messengers of love.
‘ ’Tis he thine absent thought employs
‘ I know—but tell us where is Boys ?
‘ Who, as I learn, was bidden here
‘ To join your songs and taste your cheer.
‘ To-night, perchance, he was not free—
‘ Oh ! what a roving blade is he!
‘ *Do I know whither he is gone ?*
‘ Know I where shuttle-cock will fly
‘ Which twenty maidens toss on high ?
‘ Perchance one maid ’twill light upon.
‘ John Boys for all the world I’ll back
‘ To be like bull on *chulo’s*[1] track.
‘ As rage of bull is turned anew,
‘ By *capa* bright of changing hue,
‘ Unrolled by *chulo* to his view ;
‘ So Boys—as rash to do and dare—
‘ Runs headlong after ev’ry fair,
‘ And old love leaves to chase the new.

XVII

‘ If you had e’er at bullfight been,
‘ (At Seville I the sport have seen),
‘ The force of my similitude
‘ You’d own—for by this hand, ’tis good.

---

[1] *Chulo,* the individual who distracts the bull’s attention by flourishing his coloured *capa,* which is generally of silk or satin. It is his business to rescue the *matador* or *picador,* as also the other *chulos* when hard pressed by the bull.

XVIII

' *It is not true?*—My cousin fair,
' Upon my Bible-oath I swear,
' That if you ask you soon will find
' I nothing have John Boys maligned.
' And of the fact there 's no denying
' That many a maid is for him dying.
' *Their names?* Ha! ha! go search the shire,
 ' Or count the names in Lambarde's[1] book :
' So many maids doth Boys admire,
 ' So many more he hath forsook.

XIX

' Round Fredville oak,[2] on last May-day,
 ' Sweet Lucy of the golden hair
' Was little maiden bright and gay,
 ' And now—she pineth in despair.
 ' With my two eyes I saw him dare
' To give her kisses thirty-three—
' I saw—he thought I could not see.
' I did not count them, but I guess
' He gave her rather *more* than less.
' Allowance one must make 'tis true,
' For Lucy 's scarce less fair than you,
' With tiny hands and soft blue eyes,
' Although she is but half your size.'

---

[1] *Lambarde's History of Kent*, not a new book at this period, 1633-4.
[2] Fredville oak, still in existence.

E

XX

Elizabeth the Fair well knew
  That Anthony to talk was prone ;
Did she believe that story true ?
  I do not know,—'twill ne'er be known,
I fear—like Jove's—a lady's eyes
Smile at a lover's perjuries ;
  That is—if perjuries be past,
And she the perjured one holds fast.

XXI

No comment made Elizabeth,
  No time she had to speak a word,
  For something at that moment heard
Seemed as it robbed her of her breath.

XXII

Behind Aunt Grace did a servant appear,
And whispering said in that lady's ear,
' Sir Nathaniel Finch, so please you, is here.'

XXIII

A horn without had made echo before,
Now voices and footsteps were heard at the door,
And while loudly, for room, does a pursuivant call,
Sir Nathaniel and followers entered the hall.
      At Aunt Grace
      And the vacant space
Fair Elizabeth glanced, and displeased was her face.

XXIV

Trim from his coach Nathaniel Finch had stept,
And up the hall a measured pace he kept.
Of middle stature—past the middle age—
His brow was thoughtful, and his look was sage ;
While side-locks close by barber's hand were sheared ;
Bald was his crown, and grizzled was his beard.
So slow, composed, and dignified was he
Grandee of Spain he oft was ta'en to be ;
His trunken hose of ancient cut designed
With saw-dust [1] dry capaciously were lined,
And stiffly a starched ruff his neck confined ;
White was his stocking, and as white his shoe,
With huge rosette of purest Royal Blue ; [2]
Slashed with like colour was his doublet too ;
Small hat with plume erect in 's hand appears,
Rings on his fingers, ear-rings in his ears.

XXV

Such had his garb been in long vanished days,
　　When, in the Lord Southampton's stately train,
He at the Globe [3] sat out Will Shakespear's Plays,
　　In his late Majesty King James's reign.

[1] In King James I.'s reign this was a prevalent fashion, and sub-jected the wearer, besides other inconveniences, to the risk of sad disaster, for a puncture in the hose sometimes let out the padding in continuous stream.—See *Planché's Work on Costume.*

[2] Dark blue, Oxford colour.

[3] The Globe Theatre, on the Surrey side of the river. Sir Henry

XXVI

Clothes the same cut wore fair Elizabeth's sire,
Who clapping hands bid all the rest admire :
' All hail, and welcome Sir Nathaniel Finch—
' Who from the good old fashion doth not flinch ;
' Gladly my son-in-law I greet again,
' Though I did deem him still to be in Spain.'

XXVII

Beside him when Nathaniel Finch did stand,
Sir John first kisses—and then shakes his hand :
· Here is your place,' Aunt Grace then quickly said,
When of a sudden Boys SAT DOWN INSTEAD !

XXVIII

Yes ! he had come !—ah ! she was there !—
Her own true lover !—his darling fair !
Of Boys and his mistress how can the bard
Tell of emotion which art defies ?
Joy, and fear, and love, and surprise.
   He caught her hand, and he squeezed it hard,
While, in gentle Elizabeth's beautiful eyes
   There shone an expression of tender regard.

Wotton describes a fire there during the performance of the play of
Henry the Eighth, and how one of the actors extinguished the conflagration of his own slops by pouring a bottle of ale over them.
But the ' Great Globe ' must have left more than ' a wrack behind,'
or else it was rebuilt entirely, for the name long survived.

XXIX

Love two existences seemed to absorb—
  Glad they had been at that moment to fly
Afar to bright Venus' enchanted orb,
  Or to melt in each other's arms and die ;
For they knew they were all in all to each other.
(Father and mother and sister and brother,
All the relationships tender of life,
Merge—so to speak—into husband and wife.)
The secret was out that could not be concealed,
And at the same moment was danger revealed ;
They trembled to think that their hopes might be vain,
For what Love maketh one, that will Mammon make
    twain,
And soon they might part to meet never again.

XXX

' Get up, Cousin Anthony !' whisper'd Aunt Grace,
' Sir Nathaniel Finch must now sit in your place.'

XXXI

To greet Sir Nathaniel Elizabeth rose,
  He kissed her hand, and a compliment strained
And measured he paid, while his wonted repose,
  O'er voice and manner and gesture reigned.
He bowed to Boys, whom he slightly knew—
    He kissed Aunt Grace
    (Or the paint on her face)—
To Anthony nodded, and slowly withdrew ;

And when to some others he'd courtesy shown,
By Elizabeth's mother he sat himself down.

XXXII

Boys of his sweetheart's betrothal had heard
(While he was in Flanders the thing had been done),
But Elizabeth often spoke jesting word
Of the wealthy prize which her beauty had won;
And Boys, as he saw he was favoured by her,
Permitted no scruple to trouble his breast,
From her sweet presence wished never to stir,
But basked in her eyes, while he hoped for the best.
Nor rival he thought of, nor warning did mind;
He saw she was fair, and he *felt* she was kind.
Perchance, after all, he no rival might find?
And now that the rival in substance appears,
Nor idle the danger, nor groundless his fears,
Her love at that moment made plain to his eyes,
Makes his heart to beat high, and his courage to rise.

XXXIII

The board was spread on the dais again,
Sir Nathaniel was feasted and all his train;
Believe not that Boys was neglected there,
When close by his side sat his warm-hearted fair,
Who from her purpose budged never an inch,
And seemed not to care for the presence of Finch.
And joyous were both, though the goal was not won,
For love chaseth gloom like the light of the sun.

XXXIV

He told her the tale of the damsel in green
(With the mask on her face) and the thieves in the wood;
And how he both guide and knight-errant had been,
And briefly at length thus his tale did conclude :—
' At an inn two leagues hence are the masquers bestowed:
' *I* came at a gallop the rest of the road.'

XXXV

Elizabeth warmly commended the bravery
Whereby he confounded marauding knavery,
But she said, ' That maidens who mumming go,
' Should not be frighted by latent foe ;'
And vowed ' that the masquers were pitiful elves,
' That they came not the rest of the way by themselves.'
But her thought was of Boys while she censured them so.

XXXVI

Aunt Grace
Sat still in her place,
And faint and sad was the smile on her face—
Perhaps she had knowledge of menacing woes,
And pitied that handsome young gallant—who knows ?
Aunt Grace was so near
That each word she could hear,
So Boys made demand
For Elizabeth's hand
In the dance, when of tables the hall they should clear,

And hoped when 'twas over to lead her away
To some corner retired where he something might say,
Then Aunt Grace getting up from her place went her
 way.
And the chaplain at once edges nearer to Boys
And opened discussion that something annoys :—

XXXVII

' What think you of ship-money,[1] worshipful sir ?
' They say to that impost you do not demur—
' As for me, I'm directly opposed to the thing—
' For I stand for the people, and not for the king.'
' Sir,' replied Boys, though to talk something loth,
' As for " king " and for " people "—I stand for them
 both.
' The king would have England what erst she hath been,
 ' Secure on her shores from the spite of the foe ;

---

[1] An apologist for Charles I. thus speaks of this tax :—' Did he
spend it in luxury on himself, or unprofitably to the damage of his
subjects? Was it not employed for the dignity and preservation of
the nation ? Were not the ships built therewith the strength of the
kingdom? Were we not, by means of them, become formidable to
all about us? Surely from hence it was that our merchants sailed
with more freedom at sea, and their factors did negotiate with more
success and regard abroad. Hence it was that the inhabitants of the
sea-coasts slept more securely in their beds. The worshippers of
Mahomet durst not revel so near them, nor venture to steal their
children from them,* as, alas ! of late days they have done.'—*Sim-
mons's Vindication of King Charles I.*

---

 * Twenty-six children taken at once by the Turks from off the
coast of Cornwall, July, Ann. 1645.

' And dreaded abroad—of the seas to be queen,
 ' But you and some Lords and some Commons say
  " No."
' When Parliament will not the nation defend,
' Why then, Sir, let Parliament come to an end.
' And if needful supplies it so niggardly grants—
' I say—let His Majesty *take*[1] what he wants.
' So God save King Charles, and schismatics confound!'
So saying John Boys from the chaplain turned round,
Determined for once the intruder to curb,
Who talk with his fair one seemed prone to disturb.

XXXVIII

 Just then a horn was heard to blow,
  And soon tumultuous din
 From people of the ruder sort,
 Who favour boist'rous Christmas sport,
  The masquers usher'd in,
 And scenic space was found
 For twenty knights of table-round,
 Who brunt of deadly combat bore
 Till half were stretch'd upon the floor.
But Father Christmas, pitying their pain,
Set all the slaughter'd on their legs again ;
Plum porridge and stiff brawn their paunches fill,
And strong March-beer that cures each mortal ill.

STAVE THE FIFTH.

The Song.

STAVE THE FIFTH.

The Song.

I

Hark! hark! to the cry through the hall!
' A song, a song we must have!'
' Your choice then name?'
And the answer came,
' Give us a love-ditty brave!'
A lute they hand,
And to meet the demand,
Boys is to chant them a stave.
While he proved that the concords all were true,
Quoth he in the ear
Of his mistress dear,
' The choice I do leave with you;
' But greater the pleasure of all would be
' If thou wert the singer in place of me.'

II

But Elizabeth would not choose, and vow'd
That she had not voice for so great a crowd.
' Well, here's a song I myself have made,'
Boys then presently answer'd and said:

' Cold without is the wintry scene,
   ' But this hath colour from warmer time ;
' I framed it when fields and woods were green,
   ' And who it was that inspired my rhyme
      ' I leave *her* to tell
      ' Who the truth can spell,
' But the name of the song it doth suit thee well,
      ' For I call it —

Beauty's Queen.

1

Bring all the choicest blossoms gay
   That gem the bright parterre,
A royal wreath I make to-day
   For my sweet mistress fair,
Who shines a radiant summer moon
   'Mid lesser stars serene—
Go—twine the gorgeous flow'rs of June,
   And crown her Beauty's Queen !

2

Since war of roses white and red
   Her lovely cheeks declare,
Their rival buds shall deck the head
   Of my sweet mistress fair
With rarest gifts of summer hours,
   Where Flora's hand has been.
Go—weave the diadem of flow'rs
   And crown her Beauty's Queen !

Beauty's Queen.

Allegretto.

Bring all the choic-est blos-soms gay That gem the bright par - terre, . A roy - al wreath I make to-day For my sweet mis - tress fair, . . . Who shines a ra - diant sum - mer moon, 'Mid les - ser stars se - rene; Go, twine the gor-geous flow'rs of June, And crown her Beau - ty's Queen! And crown . . her, and crown her, And crown her Beau - ty's Queen!

3

Be sure that all the buds you bind
  Breathe well their perfumes rare,
For these are emblems of the mind
  Of my sweet mistress fair ;
A charm that's more than half divine,
  In all her acts is seen—
For her the sweetest flow'rs entwine,
  And crown her Beauty's Queen !

III

Was the song approv'd ? I have but to hint
That below the salt (so I hear them say),
The tables at Barham Hall[1] to this day
Of the handles of knives still bear the dint.

IV

Who is this maiden in garb of green —
  Whose locks of golden brown
  All to her waist hang down—
That comes upon the scene
  Just as that strain was ended,
And turns from Boys that glance so keen
  On her who song commended ?

V

What dangers will not faithful love defy
If it be moved by curiosity ?

---

[1] *Barham Court* is the correct name of this place. The present structure is modern.

What pains and travail will not lovers take
When jealous pangs in their poor hearts awake ?

VI

Ah, little maid ! thou and thine uncle old
To-night on desp'rate venture faced the cold,
　　And that which heart doth feel,
　　And mask would fain conceal,
　　　By other signs is told.
While gazing on that pair she mutely stands,
Convulsive movement works her little hands ;
　　Her soft blue eyes are dim,
　　While sad she looks on him,
　　　And fainter grown,
She quits old Robin's arm, and on a chair sinks down :
‘ The tale is true then, Lucy, which we heard ! ’
Her uncle whispers.   She says not a word.

VII

They were the wand'ring masquers of the road
Whom Boys had lately seen at inn bestowed.

VIII

To Boys thus spoke his sweetheart so fair :—
‘ You invited this maiden our revels to share ? ’
‘ Nay,’ said John Boys, ‘ I did not, I swear ! ’
‘ Swear not ! ’ laughed she, ‘ 'twere no harm if you did.’

IX

To the maiden presently welcome was bid—
Would she of feast partake, and mask remove ?

She prays to be excused:
Would she her lore display, or skill as minstrel prove ?
' At first she all refused ;
But pressed again,
Saith ' She will try to recollect a strain
' If the good lady and that gallant kind
' To hear it be inclined.
' 'Twas but a harmless lay her mother taught her.'
(The lute that Boys had play'd on then was brought
her)
Her fingers trembled as they touch'd the chords,
And her voice faltered as she sang these words :—

1

When daisies' sheen
Deck'd all the green,
And flow'rs did scent the air,
While dance and song
The night prolong
Your love you proffer'd there.
Now Spring is fled,
And flow'rs are dead,
And frost doth nip the plain ;
Your heart, I see,
Is changed to me,
So take thy love again.

2

Another maid
Your vows persuade,

Who doth your fancy move ;
　As fondly true
　As I to you,
I pray that she may prove.
　Though hope be fled,
　And joy be dead,
Yet ne'er will I complain—
　Of pledge to me
　I make thee free,
So take thy love again.

3

　When all is changed
　Thy heart estranged,
No more would I control ;
　I do not care
　For half or share,
Where I would claim the whole.
　The maiden true
　Who loves but you
Henceforth you'll seek in vain ;
　So breaks the spell—
　Farewell ! farewell !
Take, take thy love again !

X

The lute is laid aside, the song is done,
Forth from the hall are niece and uncle gone ;
But when once more her small feet pressed the snow,
Behind her mask tears plentifully flow.

Lucy's Song.

Moderato.

When dai - sies sheen deck'd all the green, And

flow'rs did scent the air, While dance and song the night pro-long Your

love you prof-fer'd there. Now spring is fled, and flow'rs are dead, And

frost doth nip the plain; Thy heart, I see, is changed to me, So

take thy love a - gain, . . . a - gain, . . . So take thy love a -

- gain, . . . a - gain, . . . So take thy love a - gain!

STAVE THE SIXTH.

The Dance.

STAVE THE SIXTH.

The Dance.

I

'Let the trestles be moved !   .
'Put the tables aside ! '
Sir John to his blue-coated serving-men cried ;
Musicians the note of accordance proved,
And the gallants sought for the fair ones they loved.
Measure, pavan, or cinque-pace,[1] all ?
Or which of the three shall be danced in the hall ?
'A measure ! a measure ! ' the master commands,
While calling attention by clapping of hands.

II

Sudden a pause in the mirthful noise,
    The crowd upon either side are receding,
And down from the dais steps Master Boys,
    The peerless Elizabeth gallantly leading.

---

[1] The pavan and cinque-pace were dances of Queen Elizabeth's era ; but it is observable that the country gentry in the Caroline period did not always adopt the latest fashions of Whitehall.

He so handsome, and she so fair,
Not in all Kent were so gracious a pair.
Most knew the peril that Boys did dare,
And such was the sympathy felt in his cause
That there rose to the roof a faint hum of applause.

III

Gay-hearted Charlie and Dick of the Grange,
Humphrey the can-clinker, Timothy Strange,
With Hal of the Globe, and brave chorister Phil,
And still more especially dare-devil Will,
    Comrades of Boys,
    Did stir up a noise;
They were his friends, and by some it is said
They were quite ready the lovers to aid
If any rival their rights should invade.

IV

' Soul of my father ! ' Sir John exclaimed,
 ' Doth he come here my displeasure to brave ?
' Shall Sir Nathaniel be openly shamed ?
 ' No, let me die ! but this dance he shall have ;
' Son-in-law claim your affianced bride,
' And put the intrusive pretender aside.'

V

Sir Nathaniel Finch was a courtly knight,
 Who act of rudeness did ever decline,
And but for Sir John would have yielded his right,
 And claim to a dance to his rival resign ;

But no retreat would Sir John allow,
  So he went to the lady and made a leg,[1]
And with deferential and dignified bow,
  Her hand in that dance did presently beg.
Boys fair Elizabeth's fingers kept fast,
But never a look on her face did he cast,
His partner, who tried not to free her hand,
Refused Sir Nathaniel Finch's demand.
The well-bred knight did no anger show
As he bowed to the lady and off did go.

VI

But the father now rushed to his daughter's side,
' I will not suffer such conduct,' he cried ;
    ' This dance, as I live,
    ' To Finch you shall give.
' In mine own house I will not be defied ! '
But Boys of her hand still kept fast hold,
And his partner was true to her purpose bold ;
' I am sorry,' quoth she, ' that my father is vex'd,
' Boys hath this dance—let Finch take the next.'

VII

' Dar'st thou to answer thy father with no ?
' To thy chamber, wench, thou shalt presently go.
' Sirrah, the hand of my daughter resign,

---

[1] Lucy Hutchinson, in her ' Memoirs,' describes some person as
' an insignificant gallant that could only *make his leggs* and prune
himself.'

' For she is Finch's affianced—not thine !
' Mistress, to you my command is plain—
' I go to bring Sir Nathaniel again.'

VIII

His manner was angry, his voice was loud,
He turned away to seek Finch in the crowd.
Whisper'd John Boys to his lovely fere,
' Hearken to me, Elizabeth dear;
' When my good father's estate shall be clear
' He will give me three hundred pounds[1] a year,
' And though no title I yet can claim,
' My sword shall show me the way to fame.
' Defy thy sire, affianced, and all,
' And with thy true lover walk forth from the hall ;
' Thou art my soul, my heart, my life,
' And my dearest wish is to make thee my wife.'

IX

Her heart beat fast and her eyes grew dim,
As thus sweet Elizabeth answered him :
' With thee to live, and with thee to die,
    ' Thy wife, dear John, I promise to be ;
' But do not, I pray thee, persuade me to fly,
    ' At least, till no other help I see.'
And her strength being seemingly nearly spent,
Upon the arm of the gallant she leant.

---

[1] Equal to about 1,500*l.* per annum in the present day. The father of Colonel Boys lived till after the Restoration.

X

To Elizabeth came her mother, and spoke
  (A kind and simple matron was she) :—
' Do not your father's anger provoke
  ' When he says that Finch your partner must be.
' Is a dance, indeed, a matter so grave
' That Sir John's displeasure you needs must brave ? '
But Elizabeth did her mother withstand,
And would not let go John Boys his hand.

XI

Sir John approached his child again
With Sir Nathaniel in his train,
While all the guests did stand aghast,
And grave and anxious glances cast ;
For well they knew unwonted thing
Was at that moment happening.
Sir John, who still his temper curb'd,
    Or slave to careless jollity
    By neighbours mostly thought to be,
Had ne'er before been so disturb'd ;
And all did marvel at the change,
For wrath of peaceful man is strange.

XII

' Elizabeth,' thus spoke her sire,
  ' Take Sir Nathaniel's hand ;
' He comes again at my desire,
  ' So slight not my command.'

Then Sir Nathaniel bowed again,
But still as statue did remain
   Elizabeth the fair,
And all perceived the suit was vain;
For father's mandate, it was plain,
   The daughter did not care.

XIII

Sir John on Master Boys now turned,
While fury in his aspect burned:
' To take the place of better men
  ' Hither you were not asked,' said he,
' But never more as guest again
  ' At Barham you shall welcome be.
' Lead forth the girl, Nathaniel Finch,
  ' If she forgets each lesson taught her,
' *I* from my duty will not flinch—
  ' Stand aside, sirrah, from my daughter!'

XIV

Though Master Boys I late defined
As slow to anger—bear in mind
I meant not that his spirit slept
In calm that tempest never swept;
Where insult palpable was meant,
Keen could he feel, and fierce resent.

XV

The sound that is by organ made
Depends upon the stop that's played;

What soft as lute on ear may steal,
 Or sweet as tuneful harp may fall,
At times, like rolling thunder-peal,
 Will shake the minster's massive wall.
The spirit of John Boys was up,
And out flew battle-trumpet stop!

XVI

' Sir John,' he said, ' if lady fair
 ' With hand in dance doth honour me,
 ' That lady's partner I will be,
' No matter who the claimant there.
' But if for life the choice be made,
' And rival would my rights invade,
' The deadly combat he must prove,
' And FIGHT for her he dares to love!'

XVII

While loud his closing accents rung,
Down on the floor his glove he flung.

XVIII

 A hush, a pause;
 Again an outburst of applause,
  Which made it plain
 That younger gallants back'd the cause
  That love appeared to gain.
Ere Sir Nathaniel Finch could move
Sir John picked up his rival's glove—
' No brawling in my house,' said he;
' Who fights my guests must first fight me!'

XIX

Just then from gall'ry high
The music 'gan to sound;
With viol, harp, and hautboy ringing round,
Their power the minstrels try—
So may harmonious spell be found
And wrath be forced to fly.

XX

Well done!
The noble pair
Who cause have won,
Shall lead the measure there!
Not so; though hand in hand,
They both expectant stand,
The dance they'll never share.
Sir John looked up,
And in a voice of thunder bade the minstrels stop,
And ended was the feast.
The music ceased!
The measure loud and gay,
In wild discordant clamour died away!

XXI

So endeth dream of rapture scarce begun,
So joy doth fly when love's brief course is run,
And Mammon parts what Sympathy made one!

XXII

Not yet morning, though night speeds on,
The lovers are parted, the guests have gone :
    All is silent in Barham hall,
Where mirth, and music, and laughter rang ;
    The stars peer in through the windows tall—
Holly and ivy in darkness hang !

STAVE THE SEVENTH.

To Church.

STAVE THE SEVENTH.

To Church.

I

' To-morrow is Christmas-day,
' And the church unto all is free,
  ' At the end of the pew
  ' Is a place for you,
' And there you shall sit by me—
  ' For I care not what people say.'
Such was Elizabeth's parting word,
  And the heart of Boys it had deeply stirred,
    For now he thoroughly knew
    That he had a mistress passing fair,
    Who was as brave as true.
And often that night, though the gallant awoke,
The thought of the words which his lady-love spoke
  Had banished each thought of care.

II

  The snow, like a silver pall,
  Still over the landscape lay,

And the sun was bright
With the faint clear light
Of the short December day;
And to church go the people all,
While the summons so sweetly swells—
Though the air was chill,
It was calm and still,
And for miles you could hear the bells.

III

Dark in relief stands sepulchral stone
With its brief record of life that's done,
Blurr'd with moss, or with lichen o'ergrown;
Darker the yew and the cypress tall,
Which sadly the unknown past recall;
But lads and lasses do laugh at all—
And while all were jovial there,
What gloomy thoughts could he have,
Who boasted of mistress passing fair,
So tender, and true, and brave?
He doff'd his hat at the ivied porch,
While the organ was shaking the walls of the church;
The quire it was gaily decked with green:
Oh, what was his sad dismay!
No trace of his lady-love there was seen,
The seat was vacant that fill'd should have been;
She came not to church that day!

STAVE THE EIGHTH.

The Rival shall Win.

STAVE THE EIGHTH.

The Rival shall Win.

I

Elizabeth's aunt from her couch arose
After a few hours' brief repose ;
Last night with her chaplain she sat up late
To settle the fixed decrees of Fate ;
To them the mind of Infinity
Was as easy to read as their A, B, C.
The Apocalypse they could rightly spell,
And who was the Man of Sin could tell.
They found they had now no manner of doubt
But that Boys belong'd to a fore-doom'd rout ;
'His place,' through his nose the chaplain sings,
'Is Tophet—the region reserved for kings.'
(A stone at the Royalist thus he flings.)
And their pious hearts doth the vision warm,
Of seeing him burnt in a sulph'rous storm,
(For the horrible torments their foes shall endure
Form a pleasing prospect to saints secure).
When a suitable prayer the chaplain had said,
With a lighter heart Aunt Grace went to bed.

II

But now on the morning of Christmas-day
From the Bottomless Pit she retraceth her way,
From Tophet—a place that's reserved for kings—
She cometh up unto mundane things,
And angrily goeth to war with Fate,
Which she thinks her plans is about to checkmate.
'Tis said that at Boys she her cap once set,
And his dull response could not all forget,
And therefore did not a match approve
Where it was plain he did marry for love.
But quite at the end of her wits she stands
At the thought of Sir John and his house and lands,
And of Finch slipping through fair Elizabeth's hands.

III

Conceive the state of a spider's thought,
Who her fine web with labour hath wrought,
Beholding the fly she is plotting to seize
Breaking away from her net by degrees.
Some slight image therein you'll find
Of the state of this worthy lady's mind;
But worse was the case, since it plain could be shown
That the fly breaking loose would the spider bring down.

IV

All were in pitiful state at the hall;
Sir Nathaniel Finch he slept not at all;

Sir John he awoke most quiet and tame,
But he felt the stings of remorse and shame;
His wife—she wept, for her innocent mind
To romance of true-love was still inclined;
But pale Elizabeth did stoutly say,
That though all the household at home should stay,
She would to church upon Christmas-day.

V

Spider! spider! thine art employ,
Lest artless passion thy web destroy.

VI

Aunt Grace might boast of her manner refin'd,
And indeed like an eel she could turn and wind,
And with soft phrases and looks could cheat,
But the proper name for her art was—Deceit;
Paint on the cheek you shall presently know,
But an inward devil, all silver'd—not so.

VII

She goes to her niece and her skill employs—
  Hopes she'll forget misconstructions past,
  Professeth a friendship firm and fast,
And vows she is now in favour of Boys;
Weeps a little, and squeezeth her hand;
Hopes she will true to her purpose stand—
The woman who cares not for gold or land,
But chooseth a husband handsome and brave,
Will be sure at least contentment to have.

As for Sir John—if it be in his power,
She was sure he would give her a liberal dower.
Then she wished her joy, with caresses endearing,
And smiled—while her inward devil was sneering.

VIII

Then to the mother she goeth to prove
How Boys that maiden apparell'd in green—
    Lucy by name—did formerly love;
If in Anthony's tale any truth there had been,
    She barbs it with slander, effect to improve.

IX

With ' Say not *I* told you,' she urges her on,
And she and ' familiar' then work on Sir John;
With him she ends thus:—' You must speak now or
        never;
Reveal to her all, or thou'rt ruined for ever.'

X

Reveal?   What, then, is this mystery
Of which this janitress keepeth the key?
To a *she* St. Peter is liberty given
To lock up the golden gates of heaven?
Can Adam and Eve no paradise win
But a sad *she*-snake goeth wriggling in?
Alas! since the fall poor humanity curs'd,
She-tigers—snakes—devils—are ever the worst!

XI

The Fates who do hold a perpetual war
With the children of Earth ev'ry joy seek to mar.
Where Clotho and Lachesis, shrouded in gloom,
    The threads of our lives and our loves are entwining;
    The true-lover's-knots of the fairest designing
Are cut by the merciless Scissors of Doom.

XII

To the daughter's chamber the father hies,
Where the mother retails Aunt Grace's lies.

XIII

' Alas ! ' saith he, ' to the task I am loth,
' But I come a secret to tell you both.'
He turn'd the key in the chamber door,
And, faltering, spoke with his eyes on the floor.

XIV

' Daughter, I come to bid thee good-morrow ;
' My heart—it is fill'd with shame and sorrow ;
' To make thee amends I think it right,
' For harsh were thy father's words last night ;
' To thy friend, John Boys, I was also rude,
' But thy feelings tow'rds him I but half understood,
' And thou know'st I am something hasty of mood.'

XV

Appeased was now Elizabeth's ire,
With her arms round his neck—she did kiss her sire.

Choked was his voice as, in accents mild,
He cried, ' Heaven bless thee, my darling child !—
' Would I could grant thee thy heart's desire ! '

XVI

' Oh, wife ! oh, daughter ! a secret I tell,
' Which for three long years I have guarded well,
' (To the will of Fate we must all of us bow)
' But it grieves my heart to reveal it now.
' Wife, thy dowry is wholly spent !
   ' I have no portions my girls to give,
    ' And worse—we had not the means to live,
' If a friend had not thousands on thousands lent.
' The boys for themselves, perhaps, something may do,
' But, if that friend should be found untrue,
' I tremble, dear wife, for my daughters and you.
' Each thing that is thought to be mine by right
' Belongeth—belongeth '—here falter'd the knight—
' To a man who could claim—who could seize on all.
' For *he* did redeem lands, chattels, and hall—
' From revelation no longer I flinch—
' I OWE UPWARDS OF FOURSCORE THOUSAND TO FINCH ! '

XVII

As when by sudden flash of Wisdom's shield
The direful face of Gorgon is reveal'd,
And luckless gazers are to stone congeal'd,
So wife and child, possest of secret dread,
With frozen eyes half starting from their head,
Like marble statues stand, with hearts as dead !

XVIII

The sound of the bells is rolling
Over the landscape white with snow ;
But Elizabeth's heart is filled with woe,
And they seem for a funeral tolling !—
To the church she must not go.

XIX

' Mother, dear, from thy child begone,
' For my heart it breaks—I would weep alone ! '

XX

Sir Nathaniel Finch heard the maiden weeping—
Tears, perchance, he had shed some too,
In his chamber lone, while the rest were sleeping,
While he thought of the loss of his sweetheart true ;
But in truth she had never his heart in keeping,
For the suit that by tender of gold is won,
When it seemeth ended is scarce begun.

XXI

Her tiring-maid the tidings to her brought
That Sir Nathaniel Finch an audience sought ;
Into her chamber straightway he was led.

XXII

He came—he bow'd – he knelt—then rose and said,
' Fair one, last night too plainly it was proved
' That younger man than I thy fancy moved ;

'Too late, sweet siren, I am forced to learn
'That faithful love doth meet with no return;
'But not with hope shall my true homage end—
'Henceforth, Elizabeth, I am thy *friend!*
'Here be the parchments that should make thee mine,
'All to the fire thou shalt at once consign;
'Sir John shall give my rival back his glove,
'I shun the combat—since he hath thy love;
'And further, my sincerity to prove,
'Half of my fortune now I give to thee,
'And when I die thou shalt my heiress be.
'Farewell!—the hand I kiss which I resign—
'Thy heart is free—though prison holdeth mine.'

XXIII

The deeds he handeth, and brief writing gives
That makes her rich, whether he dies or lives.
A tear rolled down his pale and wither'd cheek,
But he had left the room ere she could speak.

XXIV

And now from below sounds the signal of starting,
And Finch and the whole of his train are departing.

XXV

As for a funeral ringing,
The bell in belfry swinging,
Now seems as it were singing,
With ruthless iron tongue:—

'Though beard and locks be ting'd with white—
'He was once a gallant brave and bright,
  'And handsome too when young!'

XXVI

In lamentation sad and sore,
  That peerless maiden, late so gay,
All listless on her chamber floor,
  Seemed she would sob her heart away!
She lay, with her tresses half veiling her form,
Like fair weeping-willow o'erthrown by the storm.

XXVII

Sermon and prayer-time are nearly sped,
Sudden the thought comes into her head,
And to her feet she rises again;
  Back she throweth her long brown hair,
And says, as she looks through the window pane:
  'He is prompt to do and dare;
'When he findeth me not in my place in the church
'He will come here for his true-love to search—
  'Who, alas! is no longer true—
    'Who, alas! can no longer love!
  'But, oh! my father, I owe it to you
    'That I now must faithless prove!
'All hope of escaping my prison is vain,
'So fast am I bound with this terrible chain
    'That I cannot a finger move.
'He will come hither to lead me away,
'Ah, pitiless fate!—I must say to him "Nay;'

H

'Her he designeth to take for his wife,
'Is sold, alas! to another for life!
'And though for the last time I look on his face,
'I must coldly receive him, and shun his embrace!
  'I would save my belov'd from pain,
    'And I know I have oft been told,
  'That a lover is quickly himself again
  'If he can but believe that his mistress is vain
    'And worthless—or false and cold.
'How deeply soever I feel the smart,
'I must hide my feelings, and steel my heart,
'While I tell him 'tis better for both we should part.

XXVIII

  'Adieu to the tender delights of love—
  'A merciless destiny ruleth above—
    'And since I can never be wedded to him,
  'A bridal garland procure for me,
  'Of pansies and cypress and rose-mary;
  'All under the chancel my couch shall be,
    'In the family vault so dim!
  'And for epithalamium, I would desire
  'The clerk to chaunt me a dirge i' the quire,
    'While the raven croaketh a hymn!'

XXIX

So saying, Elizabeth, fair and true,
  Bindeth once more her disorder'd hair—
From her eyes she washeth the pearly dew,
Which again and again breaks forth anew,
  So deep is her sad despair.

XXX

At length, by the path through the oak-woods tall,
A plum'd hat and mantle approaching she spies—
'He is here! he is here!' fair Elizabeth cries,
'And he comes by himself to the hall.'

XXXI

And now she decideth to see him alone,
To her withdrawing-room he shall be shown;
Thither Aunt Grace in some hurry had gone,
And a new Scotch paraphrase sits trying over,
Hoping some secrets just then to discover;
The spider, who mischievous web had been spinning,
Would witness the end since she made the beginning—
With eyes through the oriel stealthily peering,
She watches John Boys, who the mansion is nearing.
Elizabeth enters—yes!—there was Aunt Grace!
The passionate blood rushes into her face;
The sudden conviction each feeling o'ermasters,
That there sat the author of all her disasters!

XXXII

And all the elaborate scheming of years—
Her blandishments, smiles, and her crocodile tears,
Each word and each look in its true light appears;
The mild and angelic contriver of evil,
With the varnish rubb'd off, stands reveal'd as—the
Devil!

XXXIII

One step from the door
Fair Elizabeth made,
And then moveth no more.
' Depart from my chamber this instant ! ' she said,
And stamped her small foot on the floor—
While hatred immortal shot forth from her eyes.
The sudden command seemed her aunt to surprise,
As much as a voice from the dead ;
Her paraphrase-playing at once she gives o'er—
All pale from her seat doth the lady arise,
And then her face gloweth in patches of red ;
And though half dismayed, yet with anger she glareth,
Like wild-cat to spring on her prey that prepareth ;
And much she desires, as her faintness [1] decreases,
To fly at her niece, and to tear her in pieces !

XXXIV

' Leave the room ! ' fair Elizabeth cried out again—
' Since family honour by thee hath been sold,
' The niece and the aunt no more converse shall hold ;
' Begone ! for I never will speak to thee more ! '
Aunt Grace saw resistance was vain ;
As Parthian defieth
The foe while he flieth,
From head to foot scanning her hated niece o'er,
With a withering smile she went forth from the door,

---

[1] In the sense of ' fear.'

And when she had passed it encounters John Boys ;
  And pressing his hand,
  While his features she scanned,
The dame to herself thus her triumph enjoys :—
' He will not be able to move her an inch ;
' I know from her spite that she means to take Finch—
' How sadly the collar her withers[1] will pinch ! '

[1] ' Let the gall'd jade wince, our withers are unwrung.'—*Hamlet.*

STAVE THE NINTH.

The Love-Knot Torn.

STAVE THE NINTH.

The Love-knot torn.

I

The fire is out; though logs be charr'd
  White ashes on the hearth are lying—
  So sinketh flame of passion, dying,
By cold and cruel fortune marr'd.
On ceiling white no warmth doth glow,
Its mouldings but reflect the snow;
But, faintly all the chilly room,
The roses of last year perfume;
In jars their wither'd leaves are stored,
  Like priz'd memorials of the dead,
And mingled essence hath been poured
  Upon remains of splendour fled.
The scent of perish'd blossoms gay
Retaineth power for many a day,
To call up vision pass'd away;
And long shall Master Boys remember
The strange sweet odour of that chamber.
The clock that ticks in turret high,
  The moss-grown dial on the wall,
Measure the moments as they fly,
  Of his last visit to the hall!

II

In brave apparel's useless pride,
    Elizabeth her art employs
Her bosom's heavy woe to hide,
    While long adieu she bids to Boys.
Upon the virginals [1] she leant,
And downward were her glances bent.
From the Star Chamber of her eyes,
Which robbed her subject's liberties, [2]
The dark-fring'd hangings will not rise.
Ah! not for pride—but in despair,
Shines the trim glory of her hair,
    For sorrow her sweet brow is shading,
Her lovely cheek is touch'd with care,
    And merry England's emblem fading,
Leaves only Christmas roses there!

III

No doubt her lover bold alarms,
    'All fears are past,'
      Thinks he, 'at last!'—
O'er Persian carpet noiseless moving,
    He only sees the peerless charms
Of his sweet mistress, brave and loving,
    And hastes to clasp her in his arms:—

---

[1] The ancestor of the piano, and something like it in shape.

[2] These lines are printed in italics because they are to be found in the *Rump Ballads.*

IV

' Chill felt the church without thee, dear!
  ' In wonted place
  ' I miss'd thy face,
' But oh! what joy to meet thee here ! '

V

Stand back, John Boys, thy suit is vain!
  The Scissors keen
  Came in between,
And cut the true-love-knot in twain !—
And all his rapture turns to pain!

VI

She shuns her lover's warm embrace,
She dares not scan his changing face ;
While the blood rushes to her heart,
She coldly tells him, they must part.

VII

' Thy playmate's folly now is o'er,
' Thou know'st that I was pledg'd before ;
' Nathaniel Finch my hand doth claim—
' Doubtless my conduct some will blame—
' If mine the fault, be mine the shame.
' Though now to part we may be loth,
' Perchance 'tis better for us both ;
' And though thy face no more I see,
' I pray thee still think well of me ! '

VIII

She spoke in agitation dire,
   Trembling, but rooted to the ground—
So shakes the fair cathedral spire,
   When furious tempest roareth round.

IX

Is this his mistress true and brave!
   Is this his fancy's peerless queen!
   May not a pallid aspect mean
The slavish fears the guilty have?
The traitress, who unmasks deceit,
And driveth lover from her feet,
Full well may dread his scorn to meet.

X

But no—he cannot harshly spell
The mind of one he loves so well.

XI

To combat her resolve he strove
With moving speech, but failed to move,
And useless are the wiles of love—
Her dainty waist he may not clasp,
   (Where beateth heart so warm and true)
Her rigid hand eludes his grasp,
   (How it could toil for love, he knew)—
But why pursue the painful theme,
Where gorgeous past becomes a dream?

Or paint the pangs no tongue can tell,
Where Passion bids to Hope farewell!

XII

Ah! deep his true-love's skill was shown—
From her dear presence he is gone,
And thinks the grief is all his own!

XIII

Scarce had he passed the outer door,
When the dumb fall on chamber floor
Told that the fond deceit was o'er!

STAVE THE TENTH.

A Love-Knot Tied.

STAVE THE TENTH.

𝔄 𝔏𝔬𝔳𝔢-𝔨𝔫𝔬𝔱 𝔱𝔦𝔢𝔡.

I

All darken'd are the lover's joys—
 To see the maiden loved in vain,
 He never more returned again—
From Barham rideth Master Boys,
 While frost and snow do melt away,
And chilling show'rs began to fall,
 He looked behind at close of day—
 A rain-cloud looming dim and gray
Veil'd sadly the enchanted hall!

II

From Minster[1] windows, colours bright
Fall on the quire-men's smocks of white—
They sing for Lady Finch the Fair—
In tippet and in rochet there
The Bishop blesseth wedded pair.
But when she signed her maiden name,
A shadow o'er her features came,

---

[1] Canterbury Cathedral was at this time well furnished with stained glass ; Rochester also.

And her bright form a tempest shook,
Blotting the entry in the book.

III

My friends, I hear some murmuring
At the sad history I sing—
Doubtless the youngsters here await
A brighter end to true love's fate
(Forgetful of proverbial rhyme
Recorded by a wit sublime [1]),
And hope for some exciting tale
Of bridal marred at altar rail,
Where younger rival marcheth in
His long-expected prize to win.
Fate you must blame, my friends, not *me*,
I cannot alter destiny,
Or newly graft heraldic tree.

IV

Ere to the castle we return,
Which yet hath half its fame to earn,
Some trifles you may wish to learn.

Ah me! for aught that I could ever read,
The course of true love never did run smooth;
But either it was different in blood,
Or else misgraffed in respect of years;
Or else it stood upon the choice of friends;
Or if there were a sympathy in choice,
War, death, or sickness did lay siege to it, &c.
                    Midsummer Night's Dream, act i. sc. 1.

V

First, then, of her who love-match marr'd—
The Lady Finch's doors were barr'd
Upon the aunt with niece who warr'd.
In vain she all her art employs
On Finch—she failed once more with Boys ;
Aunt Grace soon quarrell'd with Sir John,
And when the troubled times came on,
First zealot, and then spy became ;
Some here do know the real name,
Of one who baneful influence lent
To base committee-men of Kent.[1]

VI

If aught of spinster fair and small
Your mem'ries kind can now recall,
Of her I somewhat have to say.

VII

Some time before the nuptial day,
When feast they spread, and bone-fires[2] light,
For Lady Finch and her rich knight—
A little maid, on palfrey white,
To Barham took her lonely way,
To intercede for errant knight.

[1] The candid Lucy Hutchinson, in her account of the dishonest proceedings of the Nottingham sequestrators, gives some idea of the way in which county committees abused their arbitrary powers. Plenty of evidence remains to show that the committee of Kent were not less exacting than their brethren of other counties.

[2] *Sic* frequently in diurnals of the time.

Though small her form, so large her heart,
She wept to see two lovers part,
(Of love herself had felt the smart)
But nought availed her guileless art.

VIII

Did Boys then pine his life away?
Must I reply?—then this I'll say,
I hold him scarce a man to be,
   Who cross'd in love bedews his pillow,
And robbed of shade of myrtle tree,
   Will sit and sigh beneath the willow!
Of grief did Boys become the prey?
   My friends! I thought you better knew him—
He did not to despair give way,
   But wrestling with the giant threw him.
The past, to him, was troubled dream,
Where truth and fiction mingled seem;
So from each cherished thought he flies
Of her who snared his heart and eyes.

IX

Better try gay Mercutio's cure
Than pangs of vain regret endure.

X

They say—and I believe it true—
   The night of interrupted feast,
   The inn that held him as a guest,
By chance held little Lucy too.

Her tender love for him he learns,
But, yet no flame responsive burns.
Believe me, innocent the art
By which he won that maiden's heart;
Round Fredville oak, one night in May,
   The homage Beauty doth exact,
And gallantry is bound to pay,
Spirited Lucy's heart away,
   But that of Boys left all intact.

        XI

When Finch some weeks had wedded been,
A palfrey near a church was seen,
   From which a little maid did light;
(The maiden was not dressed in green,
   Although the little steed was white)
       In choir they sing,
       Maid puts on ring,
And comes forth wife of errant knight.

        XII

Round Fredville oak we danced again—
   Some here to-night those sports did share,
   And full of jollity we were—
But we were lads and lasses then,
   And had but little thought of care.
If transient were the joys we knew,
Our griefs of old were transient too!
Elastic youth soon smiles again
At woes that crush the hearts of men.

XIII

The gale of June o'er garden sweeping
　May toss the roses in their beds,
Some petals lost—some dew-drops weeping—
　Again all fresh they raise their heads ;
But when October chills the blast,
　To earth the canker'd flow'rs are cast !

XIV

Friends, here's a toast ! fill cups and glasses—
' The days when we were lads and lasses ! '

XV

Ah ! would that we could see once more,
The free—the jovial days of yore !
We then had King and Church and Laws,
And dreamt not of the Cov'nant cause ; [1]
We had no fear of traitors bold,
While Magna Charta still did hold ;

---

[1] This complaint is supposed to be uttered about 1648. Lord Clarendon thus describes the ' temper of the nation ' at this time :— ' If a universal discontent and murmuring of the three nations, and almost as general a detestation both of Parliament and army, and a most passionate desire that all their follies and madness might be forgotten in restoring the King to all they had taken from him and in settling that blessed government they had deprived themselves of, could have contributed to His Majesty's recovery—never people were better disposed to erect and repair again the building they had so maliciously thrown down.'—*Clarendon's History of the Rebellion*, vi. 1.

No rotten Ordinances [1] then
Did bind the hands of Englishmen ;
We were not then under the Westminster knaves, [2]
Who prison the King and his people make slaves !

[1] The Acts passed by the Houses during the *interregnum* were called Ordinances.

[2] 'These are they,' says the author of *The Mystery of the Two Juntos* (published 1648), after he has shown how the ' grandees ' of Parliament and army have divided the spoils—' these are they who, with Hananiah, break the wooden yoke from off our necks and put on one of iron ; free us from a little ship-money, paid thrice in an age, and impose as much at once for a monthly tax; quit us of monopolies of tobacco, and set up an excise on bread and beer. The first caseth the wanton rich man, and the latter grindeth the needy and poor. Yet these are thy gods, oh London ! These are the idol calves the people have set up and do worship !—these be the Molochs to which you sacrifice sons and servants, by troops, regiments, and armies, to maintain their sovereignty, rebellion, and profit.'—*Mystery of the Two Juntos*, 1648.

STAVE THE ELEVENTH.

Of the Former Days.

STAVE THE ELEVENTH.

Of the former Days.

I

The former days, the former days !
  Ah, gentle friends, ne'er ask me more,
With tuneful harp, to chaunt the praise
  Of fleeting pleasures past and o'er !
The songs we sang—the pranks we play'd—
  With mirth, and jest, and laughter loud—
Are done—and many a gallant proud
  And playmate fair are lowly laid !

II

Too soon the curse of civil war
Came, all our harmless sports, to mar !
When law and order ceased to reign,
And knaves did eat up faithful men,
And all to chaos turned again ;
When sights were seen that hearts appal—
The chamber wreck'd—the roofless hall !
And church and minster pillaged all !

When brother against brother stood,
And all the realm was plunged in blood! [1]

III

Ah, sad the fate that time reveal'd—
Full many a comrade's doom was seal'd
   When standards of the King went down,
   And all was lost for church and crown
On Marston Moor and Naseby field!
On down, and plain, and waste, and hill,
Their lonely beds do others fill
Who fell [2] in dark and doubtful fray—

---

[1] 'The two Houses have sate seven years to hatch cockatrices and vipers. They have filled the kingdom with serpents—bloodthirsty soldiers, extortioning committees, sequestrators, excisemen. All the rogues and scum of the kingdom have been set on to torment and vex the people, to rob them, and to eat the bread out of their mouths. . . They have suppressed the true Protestant religion, suffered all kinds of heresies and errors in the kingdom, have imprisoned, or at least silenced, all the orthodox clergy, taken away the livelihood of many thousand families, and robbed the fatherless and the widows.'—*Declaration of Many Thousands of the City of Canterbury and Co. of Kent*, 1647.

[2] Vicars, one of the 'godly' party, moralises over the Royalist disasters thus:—

Psalm lviii. 10–11.—'*The righteous shall rejoyce when he seeth God's vengeance on the wicked, and shall wash his feet in their blood. So that a man shall say, verily there is a God that judgeth the earth.*'

'The Slaine on the King's Side.'

(Here follows a list of ninety-one persons of eminence, commencing with the Earl of Lindsay, General of the King's Forces, who fell at the battle of Edgehill. The Lord Falkland stands tenth on

And yew-trees wave
Above the grave
Of many a playmate fair and gay,
In cureless grief who pined away!

IV

The former days are vanished all—
But though so drear the shadows fall,
While fond remembrance backward flows,

the list; 'six priests slaine in Basing House' is the last entry but one.)

Vicars then goes on to say that there were 'many, yea, very many, more found slain on the places and ground where they fought, but not named or known who they were; very many buried by the enemies themselves in the places where they were slain; and very many thrown into rivers and secretly conveyed away out of the fields where they fought, before their flight and total rout; at least 140 cartloads (as was credibly related) of slain and sorely wounded carried to Oxford from Newberry first fight; many cartloads carried away and buried in ditches after Brainford fight; many also at Dorchester, and Cansham fights neare Oxford; many at Marston Moor's famous fight, and very many in other places too tedious here to recite—yea, almost impossible to be recited; besides such as being left behind in the fields where they fought, who, being stript, appeared plainly to be gentlemen and men of extraordinary worth and quality, both by their pure white skins, faire shirts, and very rich clothes, but could not otherwise be known unto us. And let the intelligent and judicious reader take this observation from this short catalogue of the thus slain of the King's party, even of those partly ignorant and partly malignant opposers of God and His most righteous cause, defended by the Parliament, viz., to see and take notice of especially the just revenging hand of God upon our kingdom's nobility and gentry, who have been the maine malignant and even athéistical opposers of a pure and thorough reformation.—*Vicars' Parl. Chron.,* 1646, p. 468.

I dream I may the past recall
   With all its joys, and all its woes—
For with the joy I'd take the pain,
So sweet to live the past again !

V

   In vain, in vain !—
      Then cease the song,
     Whose sad refrain
       Doth grief prolong—
What late began with prelude brave
In mournful cadence end must have ;
No more I may the past recall—
    And moving lays
    That sound their praise,
Are idle, vain, and useless all ;
  And can but ghosts and shadows raise
When time has thrown the sable pall
  That shrouds the light of former days !

VI

   No more, no more—
   My song is o'er !
Though gay it rang through bow'r and hall ;
   It ends with moan
   O'er pleasures flown,
While tears from faded eyes do fall !

STAVE THE TWELFTH.

The Siege of Donnington.

STAVE THE TWELFTH.

The Siege of Donnington.

I

The royal standard proud and gay
O'er ruined wall and rampart flies;
The watchful castle stands at bay,
And Covenanting might defies;
To bar the London [1] road it stands,
With culverin all pointing down,
Lest arm'd Rebellion's [2] vent'rous bands
Should reach the King at Oxford town.

[1] According to Clarendon, the castle was first garrisoned because it commanded the 'great road through which the western trade was driven to London.' The gallantry of the defenders, however, in foiling all the forces of the Parliament, converted it into a post of high strategic importance.

[2] It is to be observed that of late years writers in general, whatever their political bias may be, hesitate to use the word 'rebellion,' and designate it merely as the 'Civil War.' Buckle, however, is very outspoken. 'Our Great REBELLION,' says he, 'was the work, not of men who looked behind, but of men who looked before. To attempt to trace it to personal and temporary causes; to ascribe this unparalleled outbreak to a dispute respecting ship-money, or to

II

And nought could those within appal,
  So stout and bold was each defender—
Colonel Boys and his merry men all
  Swore they would sooner die than surrender!

III

Ladies and gallants, the stave that I sing
Is ringing with triumph achieved for the King!

IV

The fair, I do fear, will not wholly approve
Of a story that dealeth no longer in love.
Plainly I tell you, from this to the close
No longer in numbers harmonious it flows—
I talk not of cheeks of the lily and rose,
And of cares that are breaking a lover's repose—

a quarrel about the privileges of Parliament, can only suit the habits of those historians who see no further than the preamble of a statute or the decision of a judge. Such writers forget that the trial of Hampden, and the impeachment of the five members, could have produced no effect on the country unless the people had already been prepared, and unless the spirit of enquiry and of insubordination had so increased the discontents of men, as to put them in a state where, the train being laid, the slightest spark sufficed to kindle a conflagration. The truth is that the rebellion was an outbreak of the democratic spirit.'—*Buckle's Hist. of Civilisation,* i. 600. What follows in three or four subsequent pages is still more to the point. Although the writer approves of the Rebellion, he displays his usual candour.

In clamour discordant the rest must come
To roar of the cannon, and roll of the drum,
From me you'll get little but knocks and blows.
But I know that the same will the gallants delight—
Be he Round-headed churl—be he Cavalier knight,
An Englishman loveth a stand-up fight,
Wherein combatants bold do with fury lay on,
Fight dog, fight bear,[1] till the struggle be done.

V

September the 20th, 'forty-three,
Was fought the first battle of Newbury,
Where gallant Caernarvon[2] and Sunderland[3] brave
With the noble Falkland[4] did find a grave ;
When the King a mourning scarf had put on,
Boys into Packer's[5] old house is gone,
Which though fortress they call,
Was but house or hall,
Such as gentlemen lived in in olden days,
Ere we left our ancestors' simple ways.

[1] A common expression in the days of Paris Garden, when bear-baiting was in vogue.

[2] Robert Dormer, Earl of Caernarvon.

[3] Henry Spenser, Earl of Sunderland, only twenty-three years of age. He had married Waller's Sacharissa.

[4] Lucius Cary, Viscount Falkland.

[5] The King, after the battle of Newbury, retired 'to Oxford, leaving a garrison under command of Colonel Boys in Donnington Castle—a house of John Packer's, but more famous for having been the seat of Geoffrey Chaucer—within half a mile of Newbury.'—*Clar. Hist.*, iv. 237. Oxford : 1826.

An oblong building with flanking tow'rs
    Hold out could not
    Against Parliament shot
For more than perhaps some forty-eight hours;
    But Boys was told
    That the place he must hold
For his sovereign lord, King Charles,
    And being a Royalist firm and true,
    He stoutly determined his duty to do
In spite of their Puritan snarls.

VI

Experience in Flanders the colonel had bought—
He had not serv'd in the trenches for nought.
Fortifications he soon did trace;
He drew a pentagon [1] round the place;
He dug out his ditch, and he fenced his wall
With demi-lune,[2] bastion, and curtain and all.
Strong was the work, and when all was done,
He challenged the foes of the King to come on.

VII

Months thirteen they have glided away,
But Donnington Castle is standing at bay,

---

[1] See the sketch and plan of Donnington Castle in *Grose's Antiq.*, i. London: 1773.

[2] *Mascarille.*—Te souvient-il, vicomte, de cette *demi-lune* que nous emportâmes sur les ennemis au siége d'Arras?

    Jodelet.—Que veux-tu dire avec ta *demi-lune*? C'était bien une lune tout entière.—*Les Précieuses Ridicules.*

Though the Covenant lords and the Parliament men
Demand its surrender, and day after day
Assault it again and again.

VIII

Middleton [1] brought up an army good,
  And this peremptory message he sent:—
' To prevent the needless effusion of blood,
  ' You must yield up the place to the Parliament.'

IX

' To the King,' replied Boys, ' my allegiance is due ;
' Save blood as you please, but I yield [2] not to you.'

[1] Lieut.-General Middleton, sent by Sir Wm. Waller, after his defeat at Cropredy Bridge, with 3,000 horse and dragoons ' to follow the King into the West and to wait upon his rear, with orders to reduce in his way Donnington Castle. . . . But Middleton found it so well defended by Colonel Boys, who was Governor of it, that after he had lost at least 300 officers and soldiers in attempting to take it, he was compelled to recommend it to the Governor of Abingdon.'—*Clar. Hist.*, iv. 577.

[2]   '(*The Summons of Middleton.*)
            ' For the Governor of Donnington Castle.
' Sir,—I demand you to render me Donnington Castle for the use of the King (!) and Parliament. If you please to entertain a present treaty you shall have reasonable terms. My desire to spare blood makes me propose this. I desire your answer.
                        ' John Middleton.'

            ' (*The answer from the Governor.*)
                    ' For Lieut.-General Middleton.
' Sir,—I am intrusted by His Majesty's express command, and I

Then Middleton went at the place poll-mell,
 He brought up his scaling-ladders and all,
But the Royalists fought their defences so well,
 That the Roundheads were driven with loss from the
 wall.

X

Then Horton came with a larger train,
By regular siege the castle to gain ;
He mined,[1] and he sapped,[2] and he thunder'd his shot,
For twelve long days the bombardment was hot—
Such good success did his labours crown,
Three tow'rs and a part of the wall fell down.

XI

Horton sends message disdainful and proud,
 ' Quarter,' saith he, ' ye shall all be allowed,
 ' If to my forces your gates ye unlock
 ' By Wednesday morning, at ten of the clock ;

have not learned yet to obey any other than my sovereign. To
spare blood do as you please; but myself and those that are with
me are fully resolved to venture ours in maintaining what we are
here intrusted with, which is the answer of   ' John Boys.'
—*Heath's Chron.*, p. 62. London : 1676.

   [1] The ' mining ' can only have been with the view of discovering
a subterranean passage said to exist between Shaw House and Donnington Castle.
   [2] The ' sap' was probably the same process as at present, or similar to it. The gabions identical, but instead of a saproller a
mantelet on wheels was used.

' Refuse—and I pray that I never may thrive
' If I leave but one man in the castle alive ! '

XII

Boys unto Horton this answer did make :—
' Quarter [1] I neither will give nor take.'

XIII

Said Manchester's Earl, ' Though he foileth their swords,
' Yet, nevertheless, he may yield to my words,
' For I am the chief of the Parliament lords ;

[1] ' The blockade of Donnington Castle had been, when Middleton pursued his march into the West, left to the care of Colonel Horton, who for some time was contented to block it up; but then finding his summons neglected, and that they had store of provisions within, and having an addition of force from Abingdon and Reading, he resolved to besiege it, which he began to do on September 29, 1644, and made his approaches and raised a battery on the foot of the hill next Newbury, and plied it so with his great cannon that after twelve days' shooting he beat down three towers and a part of the wall, which he believed had so humbled the Governor and the garrison that they would be no longer so stubborn as they had been. And therefore he sent them another summons, in which he magnified "his own clemency that prevailed with him, now that they were even at his mercy, to offer them quarter for their lives if they gave up the castle before Wednesday at 10 of the clock in the morning; but that if his favour was not accepted, he declared in the presence of God that there should no man among them have his life spared." The Governor made himself merry with this high and threatening language, and sent them word "he would keep the place, and neither give nor receive quarter."'—*Clar. Hist.,* vol. iv. p. 578. The message and answer are given at length in *Cattermole's Hist.,* 138.

'The Covenant [1] plot I did help to contrive,
'And was colleague and friend of the members [2] five.'

XIV

But though his rebellion a coronet bore,
The answer of Boys was the same as before.
'Ho! ho!' quoth the Earl, 'since he willeth it so,
'This colonel malignant my fury shall know.'

XV

Dragooner and musqueteer
From Reading[3] all forth are gone,
In scarf and with bandolier,
The sun on their helmets shone.

---

[1] 'The Covenant,' says Roger L'Estrange, 'was a sort of rebellious combination made among the Scots formerly, be of what religion they would, insomuch that had these beasts entered the ark it would have puzzled Noah to have sorted them in pairs.' (!)—See his notes to *Hudibras.*

The Solemn League and Covenant was taken by the Lords and Commons, September 25, 1643. The instrument was thus headed :— *A Solemn League and Covenant for Reformation and Defence of Religion, the Honour and Happiness of the King, and the Peace and Safety of the three Kingdoms of England, Scotland, and Ireland.*

[2] Hampden, Hollis, Hazelrig, Pym, and Strode. This Earl of Manchester was at that time Lord Kimbolton.

[3] 'The Earl of Manchester hasteneth with his godly army, which God hath always made victorious, to joyn with Sir William Waller.' —*Perfect Occurrences of Parliament*, from September 20 to 27, 1644. This—which of course is from a *Diurnal* on the Parliament side— seems to refer to the Earl's advance to Newbury.

With partizan, pike, and spear,
Lord Manchester's men came on!
A victory there
Hoping to gain,
With a psalm and a pray'r,
And a battering-train,
For they thought to lay Donnington low as the ground,
And like Jericho's wall,
That the castle would fall
At the Puritan trumpet's sound!

XVI

Hark! in the castle full loud is the din,
While out-guard and piquet are all running in;
Smartly they answer the Governor's call,
And to their posts all his merry men go;
Some run with bullet and match to and fro,
Saker[1] and culverin others point low,
Making all ready to meet the foe,
With bang for bang, and with blow for blow,
While loud rings the trumpet on Donnington wall.

XVII

The trampling of feet and the rolling of wheels,
While drum, pipe, and clarion discordant are sounding,
And pennon on pennon advancing—reveals
That foemen the castle again are surrounding.

[1] A piece of ordnance.

XVIII

A pause, as a cornet [1] of horse draweth nigh,
A bandrol of white he is raising on high,
   While the trumpet shrill pealed,
   Cornet asks if they yield,
But a cheer from the walls is the only reply.

XIX

An hour passes by, and yet nothing is done :
Quoth Boys—' By St. George they do fear to come on.'
   It was just as he said,
     For the task was so warm,
   They refused to be led
     The defences to storm,
And they pointed their guns at the castle instead,
And scarcely the word had the Governor spoken
When the long silence was suddenly broken.

XX

Fire flashed from below, in thick clouds rose the smoke,
And roar upon roar all the echoes awoke,
Tossed back to the walls from the stems of the oak. [2]

---

[1] Cornet is used to denote the colours of horse, as well as the officer who carries them.

[2] ' Nor are we to overpass the memorable trees which so lately flourished in Dennington Park, near Newbury, amongst which three were most remarkable from the ingenious planter and dedicator (if tradition hold) of the famous bard Geoffrey Chaucer, of which one was called the King's, another the Queen's, and a third Chaucer's

From minion and mortar-piece service was hot ;
In show'r after show'r flew grenadoe and shot ;
Like hailstorm of Egypt the tempest did fall,
But Boys and his men being scarce touched at all,
Did laugh under cover of rampart and wall.

XXI

The fire slacken'd not for some thirty-six hours,
Then called out the warder on one of the tow'rs—
' To the other side they are shifting the train,
' And fast by the sap are advancing again ! '
Then Boys sallied out at the head of his men ;
He charg'd them with fury and fought them so hard
That out of the trenches he beat their guard,
And slew the men while the works he marr'd.
Their chief master gunner, shot right through the head,
Was there with the rebel commander left dead ;

oak. The first of these was fifty foot in height before any bough or
knot appeared, and cut five foot square at the butts, and all clear
timber. The Queen's was felled since the wars, and held 40 feet
excellent timber, straight as an arrow in growth and grain, and
cutting four foot at the stub, and near a yard at the top. . . .
Chaucer's oak, tho' not of these dimensions, yet it was a very goodly
tree. . . . This account I hadd of my most honoured friend,
Phil Packer, Esq., whose father was proprietor of the park.'—
Evelyn's Sylva, 166.

Godwin, in his *Life of Chaucer*, suggests that Chaucer only *named*
the oaks. He quotes Leland, Camden, Speght, Ashmole, and Grose,
to prove that the great poet inhabited Donnington Castle. It cer-
tainly belonged to Chaucer's son. I think Fuller says that Thomas
inherited lands near it from Geoffrey. But see *Worthies of Newbury*.

While Boys, with small loss, got back into the place
With more than one trophy the triumph to grace.

XXII

So Manchester's onslaught and vengeance intended
Like Jeremy Horton's and Middleton's ended,
For though he renewed his artillery fire,
And batter'd the walls, he at length did retire,
No longer at Newbury caring to stay
While the Royalist forces were coming that way,
And Essex' new levies in London still lay.[1]

[1] 'The Earl of Manchester himself, with his forces, came to Newbury; and receiving no better answer to his own summons than
Horton had done before, he resolved to storm it the next day. But
his soldiers, being very well informed of the resolution of those
within, declined that hot service, and plied it with their artillery
until the next night, and then removed their battery to the other
side of the castle and began their approaches by saps, when the
Governor made a strong sally and beat them out of their trenches,
and killed a lieutenant-colonel who commanded in chief, with many
soldiers; shot their chief cannoneer through the head, brought
away their cannon-baskets' (gabions) 'and many arms, and retired
with very little loss. Yet the next night they finished their battery,
and continued some days with their great shot, till they heard of the
approach of the King's army; whereupon they drew off their ordnance, and their train-bands of London being not yet come to them,
the Earl thought fit to march away to a greater distance, there
having been in nineteen days above 1,000 great shot spent upon the
walls without any other damage to the garrison than in beating down
some of the old parts thereof.'—*Clar. Hist.*, iv. 578.

A letter in the *London Post* about this time talks of the siege as
follows: 'Sir,—These are to certifie to you that Sir Miles Hobart's
regiment is here at Newbery, where we had almost brought Don-

XXIII

The King from the West with his army had come
When damp was the wind upon Salisbury Plain,
But mute was the trumpet and muffled the drum
Though he was returning in triumph again.
For Donnington, Basing,[1] and Banbury[2]
Relieved His Majesty know must be,
   And relief he had promised to bring,
And Waller[3] at Andover meant to surprise—

nington Castle down to the ground by the active endeavours of General Adjutant-Colonell (*sic*) Horton. But Lieut.-General Brown called him and his force away, and the gunnes are taken off and carried to Reading, and here is only one regiment and some of Col. Montague's and 2 or 3 troops of horse; yet we keep them in the castle, and if we might have gunnes and furniture (!) I would undertake we could have the castle in a week. . . . . The town of Newbury and the county adjacent cry out they must fall if we go and let the castle stand. I wish the committee were well informed concerning it. I daresay it is a place of such consequence as they would not lose the opportunity to gayne it, considering it is sore battered, and one breach in it that many may enter abreast. Truely two or three fireballs or granadoes shot into it would make it ours. The Lord guide the State, and be with you and us all. Yr humble servt., R. F.' (Q. Fogge?)—*London Post,* October 23, 1644.

   [1] Basing House, defended with great bravery and pertinacity by the Marquess of Winchester, its proprietor, a staunch loyalist.

   [2] Banbury, most gallantly defended by young Sir William Compton. son of the Earl of Northampton who fell at Hopton Heath. Sir William Compton never went to bed during the whole siege.

   [3] Another flight of the Parliamentary General is thus alluded to:—

Though quickly the Parliamentarian flies,
He hardly escapeth the king.[1]

XXIV

While the shadows of evening were closing o'er him—
With his royal guards behind and before him—
With the Lord George Goring,[2] and generals all,
King Charles came riding by Donnington wall,
While the lights did twinkle in Newbury town.

XXV

' Odds' wounds ! ' cries Goring, ' the standard is down[3]—

> ' Great William the Con.
> So fast he did run
> That he left half his name behind him.'
> —See *Rump Ballads.*

Sir William's own account is as follows :—' It was a great mercy of God, when the King came suddenly upon me with his whole army at Andover, and I had nothing but a mere body of horse and dragoneers with me, I made a faire retreat to Basing-stoke.'—*Sir W. Waller's Recoll.*, 712. Waller got the name of William the Conqueror because he struck one of the first blows against the King, by taking Portsmouth, which Goring shamefully neglected to defend.

[1] ' His Majesty had a great desire on his march to Oxford ' (after the capitulation of Essex's men in the West) ' to relieve Donnington Castle and Basing . . . . and then to send a good party to relieve Banbury . . . . The King came to Salisbury upon the 15th October, when he understood that Waller lay at Andover with his troops . . . 3,000 horse and dragoons . . . . They ' (*i.e.*, the King's army) ' came within four miles of Andover before Waller had any notice of their motions.'—*Clar. Hist.*, iv. 575.

[2] General of the horse since the removal of Wilmot.

[3] About this time Colonel Boys—probably ' in scorn ' of General

'One half of the castle's a heap of stone—
  'Boys he hath either surrender'd or fled!'
When lo! upon ruin of curtain and tow'r,
In gallant defiance of Parliament pow'r,
Colonel John Boys and his merry men all
Gave the King three cheers upon Donnington wall.
  'You were wrong, you see, Goring,' His Majesty said.

XXVI

And the King did quarter in Newbury,
  (Though small provision he there obtained
  For the Covenant forces the place had drained)
But there all his army stationed must be
While he sends relief unto Banbury.
But first he did ride to the top of the hill,
And great admiration his bosom did fill
When he saw how the place had held out for the crown,
Though the walls and the tow'rs were so much batter'd
    down,
And the breach[1] in the same ten foot wide at the least,
Wherein four or five men could have enter'd abreast.
And there, while the chiefs of the army stood bare,
The King ordered Boys all the facts to declare
  Of the triumphs his prowess had won.
'Kneel down,' said the King, when the story was done—

Brown, the Governor of Abingdon, who had been 'a wood-monger'—
appears to have suspended a *fagot* over the wall with a torn Parliament flag hanging to it.—See *A Diary or Exact Relation, &c.,*
October 10 to 17, 1644.
  [1] It had been made by 36-lb. shot.—See *Symond's Diary.*

King Charles laid his rapier his shoulder upon,
And Colonel John Boys he did rise up Sir John.[1]

XXVII

Much commendation His Majesty made,
And all the King's council their compliments paid,
But the Lord George Goring he privily said,—
' Sir John, a good firkin of claret or two
' 'Twould give me much pleasure to share with you,
' To drink confusion to Roundhead crew.'

XXVIII

We have all heard of Lord Goring's renown,
Rivers of liquor his throat have gone down ;
Once while he poured out his bumpers high
He let half the army of Essex go by.[2]

---

[1] 'When the King came to Newbury the Governor of Donnington attended him, and was knighted for his very good behaviour.'—*Clar. Hist.*, iv. 579. 'His Majesty knighted Sir John Boys upon the hill.'—*Symond's Diary*, p. 161. He was also promoted to the rank of full colonel.—*Sir E. Walker's Hist. Discourses.*

[2] This occurred two months before, at Lestithiel. Sir William Balfour, with the whole of the Earl of Essex's horse, 'at about three in the morning, passed with great silence between the armies' (the King's and Prince Maurice's). 'The notice and orders' (to attack) ' came to Goring when he was in one of his jovial exercises, which he received with mirth and slighting those who sent, as men who took alarms too warmly, and he continued his delights till all the enemy's horse were passed through his quarters.'—*Clar. Hist.*, iv. 546. Lord Geo. Goring was one of the very worst of the King' party. See his character as drawn by Clarendon.

XXIX

But hark ! from afar soundeth trumpet and drum,
Disturbing Lord Goring his wassail—
For lo ! the new army of Essex has come
To menace the king and the castle !

XXX

My friends, I cannot the chronicler be
Of the second great battle [1] of Newbury,

[1] October 27, 1644.—'Though the relief of Banbury succeeded to
wish, yet the King paid dear for it soon after. The very day after
that service was performed, Colonel Urrey, a Scotchman, who had
formerly served the Parliament, and is well mentioned in the
Transactions of the last year for having quitted them and performed
some signal service to the King, had in the West, about the time the
King entered into Cornwall (in a discontented humour which was
very natural to him), desired a pass to go beyond the seas, and so
quitted the service ; but instead of embarking himself, made haste
to London, and put himself now into the Earl of Manchester's
army, and made a discovery of all he knew of the King's army, and
a description of the persons and customs of those who principally
commanded ; so that, as they well knew the constitution and weak-
ness of the King's army, they had also advertisement of the Earl of
Northampton's being gone with three regiments of horse to the relief
of Banbury. Whereupon, within two days after, all their forces
which had been under Essex and Waller being united with Manchester (with whom likewise the trainbands of London were now
joined, all which made up a body of above 8,000 foot, the number of
their horse being not inferior) advanced towards the King, who had
not half that number before the departure of the Earl of Northampton, and staid still at Newbury, with a resolution to await the
return of that Earl, that he might do something for Basing, not
believing that the enemy would be so soon united.'—*Clar. Hist.*,
iv. 581.

L

Or discourse you of Urrey his treachery,
Whereby the king's army was nearly undone,
Since the bulk of the horse were to Banbury gone.
You know by surprise King Charles was taken,
Though the army's valour remained unshaken.
Nought can I say of defenders bold
Who the house of Doleman at Shaw[1] did hold,
And murdering pieces[2] and matchlocks plied
Between the shafts of the windows wide,
Or with butts of their muskets did beat back the foe
From the ramparts where Doleman's young cedar-trees
    grow;
Nor of Lisle[3] and his charge for the king and the queen;
      Nor of Cansfield[4] the brave,
      Who the army did save

---

[1] ' 1,200 horse and 3,000 foot advanced with great resolution upon Shaw House and the field adjacent, which quarter was defended by Sir Jacob Astley and Colonel George Lisle, and the horse by Lieut.-Colonel Page. They came singing of psalms, &c.'—*Clar. Hist.*, iv. 582. See also *Ludlow's Memoirs*, i. 130, 1698.

[2] 'Leather guns and key-shot,' says Captain Gwyn, in *Military Memoirs.* I suspect these to be the *case of drakes* that I find mentioned about this time.

[3] Colonel Sir Geo. Lisle, shot by order of Fairfax after the surrender of Colchester, 1648.

[4] 'The Queen's Regiment of Horse, commanded by Sir John Cansfield, charged them (Waller's horse) with so much gallantry that he routed that great body. . . . If Sir John Cansfield had not in that article of time given them that brisk charge . . . . the King himself had been in very great danger.'—*Clar. Hist.*, iv. 583. The motto on Sir John Cansfield's banner was from the 101st Psalm, 'Fiat pax in virtute tua.'—*Estrenne's Mottos and Devices.*

When Waller came over the river to Speen,
    And through the left wing
    Made a drive at the king,
Though Donnington castle did thunder between.

XXXI

Profitless was the result of the day ;
No longer the king can in Newbury stay,
By the light of the moon he is marching away,
Leaving his train and his wagons and all
Parked under cover of Donnington wall.[1]

XXXII

The royal army to Oxford is gone,
    And to Bath the king
    Is riding to bring
His Highness's [2] horse—for he meaneth again
To return to the castle [3] and pick up his train ;

[1] 'It was a fair moonlight night (27th October, 1644) . . . .
About 10 o'clock all the army, horse, foot, and cannon, upon the
King's orders, drew forth their several guards to the heath about
Donnington Castle; in which they left most of their wounded men,
with all their ordnance, ammunition, and carriages. . . . . By the
morning all the army, foot as well as horse, arrived at Wallingford,
where, having refreshed a little, they marched to Oxford.'—*Clar.
Hist.*, iv. 583.

[2] Prince Rupert. He had been ordered up before, but was not
ready to march. The King, accompanied by Lord Capel and others,
rode fifty miles before 4 o'clock the next day.

[3] It must be noted that the King had failed to relieve Donnington
Castle, which was now very short of provisions. The King himself could get no provisions, for the Parliament forces had hedged
him in.

So Colonel Sir John
Once more is alone,
For the king could leave nothing but wounded men.

XXXIII

A little bird did inform Sir John
That as soon as the king and his army were gone,
Manchester's Earl would with fury lay on,
For his army was three times as great as before:
And the knight, taking care
For defence to prepare,
His works that were damaged did try to restore.

XXXIV

But hunger will conquer the bravest of men;
Of ammunition want there was not,
But can a man live upon powder and shot?—
Would that the king were returning again![1]

---

[1] Whoever will minutely examine cotemporary writings, as well
as the scene of the occurrences here described, will, I think, admit
that there is some truth in this Royalist 'story.' I take this opportunity of thanking Dr. Palmer, F.S.A., of Newbury, who kindly
assisted my researches, affording me important information. When
his *Memoirs of Jack of Newbury* appear, the neighbourhood will become better known. In the meantime, Mr. Godwin's little work,
The Worthies and Celebrities of Newbury, will be found instructive.

STAVE THE THIRTEENTH.

The Last Assault.

151

STAVE THE THIRTEENTH.

The last Assault.

I

It was near Allhallows tide,[1] they say—
  When the cock crew loud and shrill,
  And frost was white upon heath and hill,
Alone the brave little garrison lay,
For the king and his army had all gone away.
Hark! R-r-rat-tat-tat! on the drum,
  And tara, tan, tara! on trumpet sounded;
Pennon and banner do flaunting come,
  Donnington Castle once more is surrounded!

II

Well might the prospect the Colonel dismay!
But Boys his companions are faithful men—
  Some of them well-to-do fellows of yore,
  And some of them might be the same once more,
If the king could enjoy his own again.
Poor though they be, they are honest and true;

[1] October 28, 1644.

None of your Presbyterian[1] blue
  Soldiers that gaunt city preachers have sent
  For to make wider the kingdom's rent,
  Raised by the thimbles and bodkins lent
  For a cozening promise of eight per cent;[2]—

[1] That this was a distinguishing colour of the Parliamentary party may be gathered from the description of Butler's hero :—

> ' For his religion—it was fit
> To match his learning as his wit.
> 'Twas Presbyterian *true blue*;
> For he was of that stubborn crew
> Of errant saints, whom all men grant
> To be the true Church militant;
> Such as do build their faith upon
> The holy text of pike and gun,' &c.

The Scotch, in these days, were called ' blew-caps.' Hence possibly the colour was affected by the country party as associated with the Scottish origin of ' the Covenant.' Hence, perhaps, also the modern slang term used to stigmatise those who imitate the Puritans in matters of religion.

It is to be remarked that when the Presbyterian party found that the power of the state was slipping out of their hands into those of the Independents, they generally joined the Royalists; but it was then too late. Clement Walker, a Presbyterian, is the most unsparing castigator of ' the Derby House' and the Roundheads. See what Buckle calls his ' curious' book, *The History of Independency*, which was first published when the whole country rose against the oppression of the usurping powers (May, 1648).

[2] 'The faithful,' as soon as it was decided to make war upon the King, in 1642, were stirred up by the city preachers and others. The army of the Parliament was commonly known as the ' thimble and bodkin' army, because so many women contributed any little article of plate in their possession. Plate came in in abundance.

But poor, and ragged, and true, are they,
Serving for loyalty rather than pay;[1]
  Cornet, Lieutenant, and Captain, their style,
  And more than a score of them rank and file;
      Nine or ten
      They were Kentish men,
Friends of the Colonel in former day:
Gay-hearted Charlie, and Dick of the Grange,
  Hal of the Globe, and brave chorister Phil,
Humphrey 'the can-clinker,' Timothy Strange,
  Robert of Farningham, Dare-devil Will ;—
To name you the others, I cannot now stop,
Too much of time would their titles fill up ;
Though nothing but horse-flesh of late they had eaten,
And little of that—they hoped not to be beaten,
Though the whole Parliament army did threaten.

III

All was prepared for the combat's shock,
And it was something past ten of the clock,
When the warder sung out from the barbican wall,
' The castle is now encompassèd all,
' And a trumpeter cometh with flag of white,
' With him approacheth some Parliament knight,

Eight per cent. was promised, but the lenders lost both principal and interest.—See *Echard's Hist.*, p. 535-6.

[1] The King's forces, being supported by voluntary contribution, were but poorly paid. The use of the term 'ragged' may be objected to, but campaigning soon reduces smart uniforms to that condition. The pay of the Parliament forces was very good, especially that of the officers.

' And a gross fat man, in scull-cap and gown,
' Whom I do for a Covenant preacher set down.'

IV

Now a parley soundeth—' Within there, ho !
' Please you to let the Governor know
' With the Earl of Brentford[1] speech we would hold.'

V

The same was unto the Governor told—
Came the reply with a tap on the drum :
' Blindfold within the place ye may come.'

VI

The Earl of Brentford got hurt i' the head
At the recent great battle of Newbury :

VII

' What the plague, Colonel Boys, do they want here
    with me ? '
Quoth the Earl when the two by his pallet were led.
When the napkins[2] off from their eyes did fall
'Twas seen that their checks were as white as the wall.

---

[1] A Scotchman, Earl of Forth, created an English peer by Charles I. He is as often called General Ruthyn as Ruthven. He was recently the King's General-in-Chief, but superannuated and succeeded by Prince Rupert. He was made Chamberlain to the Prince of Wales, and retained in the Council at Oxford to quiet the susceptibilities of the Scotch.—*Sabran*, p. 273. 5,460 *Addl. MSS. Bh. Museum.*

[2] This blindfolding was, of course, a common precaution. A Par-

VIII

'What! Urrey with rebels?' Lord Brentford he cried.
'I was prisoner [1] taken,' false Urrey [2] replied.
Boys in the meantime the 'gross fat man'
Scanned, and to recollect him began;

liamentary *Diurnal*, when the King's affairs were not prospering,
relates that an envoy to Oxford, from the Parliamentary party, was
not '*hoodwinked* going in,' whence was drawn an unfavourable
augury of Royalist hopes.

[1] Not mentioned by Clarendon, but asserted by *Mercurius Civicus*
and other diurnals at this time—for instance, *Weekly Account*,
October 2 to 9, 1644. The former states that 'Col. Urrey, formerly
employed by the Parliament and afterwards deserting them, was
brought up before the Committee of both kingdoms (who sat all day
very close) before whom the substance of his examination then taken
was to this effect: That he, being desirous to desert His Majesty's
service, obtained leave of His Majesty to travel into Denmark, and
for his more secure passage sought to procure a pass from the Lord-
General' (Essex), 'but before he could obtain it he, with other pri-
soners, was surprised by Sir William Waller.'

[2] Colonel Urrey, or Hurry (?) The name is met with spelt both
ways. It is to be regretted that no philologist appears to have investigated the history of missing and supplementary aspirations.
The cockney dialect must surely be of respectable antiquity. Does
the use of the indefinite article *an* indicate anything? We should
be sorry to suppose that the translators of the Bible took liberties
with the letter *h*, and yet we find—an horse, an husband, an hand-
maid, an heart, &c. I am convinced that these supposed cockneyisms
are to be traced to the Norman invasion. The lords and knights
whose names figured on the Battle Abbey roll were vanquished by
ws and *hs*. Sabran, the French Ambassador, in 1644, talks about
Vinchelsea and *Basin-ous* (Basing-House).

Ten years back did his face recall—
'Twas the quondam chaplain of Kentish Hall !

IX

' Now,' said the Earl, ' what the plague do ye want ?
' Am I in condition great favours to grant ? '

X

' To me,' quoth the chaplain, ' the Lord hath revealed
' That unless ye the castle shall presently yield— '

XI

' With revelation I nought have to do,'
Said the Earl, interrupting—' Come, Urrey, speak you,
' If still to the king ye be loyal and true ! '

XII

' Essex is sick,' Urrey answered and said ;
' Waller and Manchester[1] send me to say,
' That you, my Lord Brentford, may safe march away
With the honours of war, if this castle you'll yield
' To the army which now is drawn up in the field.'

XIII

With hot indignation Earl Brentford grew red,
And, sick as he was, started up in his bed.
' There is the Governor, sirrah,' saith he ;
' What the divil d'ye mean by thus prating with me ? '
Quoth the earl, with his fist his old truckle-bed banging,
' Sir John, Colonel Urrey is worthy of hanging—

---

[1] *Clar. Hist.* iv. 589.   The most curious account of the siege is to be found in the *Arch^a. Cantiana.*

' I very much doubt if still loyal he be ! '
Paler grew Urrey.   ' By usage of war
' The lives of all spies ever forfeited are.'
And here the fat chaplain resumed his haranguing:

XIV

' Colonel John Boys, hear the word of the Lord—
' All in this place shall be put to the sword
' Who at this time my commandment despise '—
    But here he did stop, for Boys said to his men,
' Tie me the bandages over their eyes,
    ' And march them both forth of the castle again !'

XV

    As skilful hunters gather round
    With caution, when the prey is found,
    So do the Cov'nant legions all
    Approach the leaguer'd castle wall;
    Nearer and nearer do they come,
    While train-bands march to fife and drum,
    Or psalms in dismal chorus hum ;
        Compactly move the blocks of spears,
    In ' back,' and ' breast,' and steel-cap[1] bright ;
            And on each flank,
            In eight-deep rank,
    With lighted match, the musqueteers[2]

---

[1] The steel cap was commonly called ' a pot.' The ' back ' and ' breast ' signify the two parts of the cuirass, which was similar to that worn by the Life Guards at present.

[2] A stand of pikes was always protected by matchlock men on the

Seem all prepared for stubborn fight;
And here and there, the gaps between,
Appear the drake and culverin;
While all in rear the horse are seen,
With many an ' Ironside,' be sure,
Scarred in the fight at Marston Moor.[1]
    Now plain appear
    As they come near
The city's newly-raised brigade,
Reg'ments of yellow, blue, and red,[2]
    In brand-new buff and bandolier,
Stout Londoners on capons fed,
By Sir James Harrington are led.
And all the banners floating there
Show brave device, or legend fair
Of battle-cry, and text from Word,
Which curse the king[3] but praise the Lord.

---

flanks. See the bird's-eye view of Naseby fight in *Sprigg's Anglia
Rediviva* by Nathl. Fiennes.

[1] Marston Moor was fought the previous summer.

[2] *Rushworth*, vol. v. p. 719. The *yellow* regiments, trainband of
Southwark, the *yellow* auxiliaries of the Tower Hamlets, *red* and
blue brigades of the City of London, &c.; in all 5,000 men. The
cost was 22,000*l.*

[3] So cautious, however, were most of the leaders of the Parliament army, that some of the banners of regiments intended for the
destruction of the King's armies bore loyal devices. For instance,
that of Lord (Fern^do) Fairfax, ' Viva el Rey y muera el mal go-
bierno,' which, however, was that of the revolutionary band of Masa-
niello. Sir Thos. Fairfax and Cromwell, after the establishment of
the ' new model,' adopted plain colours, without either motto or

XVI

Halt! sounds from trumpet and from drum,
No nearer Manchester will come.

XVII

Dare-Devil Will, who through loop-hole spied,
To another comrade presently cried;
' What! another knock to a partisan tied?
' While a dozen of generals round it ride.
   ' Cowards! why do they tarry so long?
   ' If I had a force but one half as strong
' The assault ere this I had tried.'

XVIII

   ' Stand, or I fire!' the sentry cries,
   So near the flag of truce now flies;
   Then pauseth he who pennon bore,
      And Ireton's face is seen,
   With Cov'nant leaders half a score
      Of dark and haughty mien.
Their trumpeter soundeth an echoing call,
And Boys and his merry men look from the wall;
And cold-blooded Ireton approacheth so near
That all in the castle his message can hear.

---

device.—See *Estrenne's Art of Making Devices*, 1650. The Parliament pretended to fight *for* the King. Doubtless many were at first deceived by this pretence.

XIX

' Ye Royalist daws!' [1]
 He them all thus addressed,
' To THE LORD and THE CAUSE
' You must yield up your nest;
' But, if you shall slight our command,
 ' Your walls we will pound
 ' Till they fall to the ground,
' And no stone on another shall stand!' [2]

XX

' Of the castle's repair,'
 Thus did Boys make reply,
' My Prince has the care;
 ' All his foes I defy;
' And if God his good aid to me bring,
 ' Although ev'ry stone
 ' Of the walls be o'erthrown,
' Yet THE GROUND I WILL KEEP FOR THE KING!'

[1] The reader will recall the saying attributed to John Knox, 'Pull down the nests and the rooks will depart.'

[2] 'The next day, when they knew that the King's army was retired, but not till then, they made haste to possess themselves of Newbury; and then drew up their whole army before Donnington Castle, and summoned the Governor "to deliver it to them, or else they would not leave one stone upon another." To which the Governor made no other reply than "that he was not bound to repair it; but, however, he would, by God's help, keep the ground."' —*Clar. Hist.*, iv. 589.

XXI

'Hurrah!'
Springing up upon rampart and wall,
His men hailed the speech with applause,
    With their caps in the air, and then one and all
Cried, 'Down with the Covenant Cause!'

XXII

The words of that Governor, faithful and brave,
And the bold response that his merry men gave,
Long in remembrance our children shall have,
    When we to ourselves are true;
When the old flag flies once more at the main,
And the ship of state shall have righted again,
    Discharging her Roundhead crew. ·

XXIII

When sudden uprose all the Royalist garrison,
Hat and feather and steel-cap waving,
Covenant menaces gallantly braving,
    On parapet, curtain, and tow'r—
Desborough, Ireton, Cromwell,[1] and Harrison,

---

[1] I see no reason to suppose that any of these heroes were elsewhere at the time of this summons and subsequent assault of Donnington Castle. The 7,000 horse that went in pursuit of the King after the second battle of Newbury must have returned a few hours afterwards. They did not leave for Blewbury till Thursday—probably after the last assault had failed.

All in amazement opened their eyes,
And some for an instant feared a surprise
And looked for a small-shot shower;
While the loud huzza did so suddenly sound
That some of their chargers did wheel right round.

XXIV

Remorseless Ireton, he heard and saw,
And in blank amazement he dropped his jaw;
  Though armèd force cometh process to aid,
  He sees the ejectment cannot be made;
And all his knowledge of logic and law [1]
  At fault is completely found:
    Though the roof and the wall
    Of the house down fall,
  Yet the tenant will keep the ground!

XXV

Ireton hath nought to reply, 'tis plain,
To the Parliament lines they all gallop again.
After some further and long delay,
Never you'd guess what they next did say;
Of former demands they have made revision—
Boys may surrender on composition! [2]—
And, lastly, 'all in the castle that are
'May march away with the honours of war—

---

[1] It will be remembered that the celebrated Henry Ireton, Commissary-General of Horse to the Parliament forces, and afterwards Lord Deputy for Ireland, was by profession a lawyer.

[2] Articles of Agreement.

' Free to pass through all posts surrounding,
' Arms in their hands, and their trumpets sounding,
' With colours flying, and matches lighted.'
But all their concessions the Governor slighted :
' This castle I hold,' said he, ' do not doubt of it.
' Till THE KING ¹ tells me that I must go out of it.'

XXVI

' Your blood, then, be on your head ! '
  Such were the last words Ireton spoke.
Nothing in answer the Governor said ;
  But a laugh did echo from Chaucer's oak.²

XXVII

While back to the lines did the white flag go,
The garrison learneth the spite of the foe.
Whiz ! went a seventeen-pounder ³ ball
At St. George's banner on Donnington wall ;

¹ ' Seeing his obstinacy they offered him " to march away with the
arms, and all things belonging to the garrison," and when that
moved not, that he should "carry all the cannon and ammunition
with him ;" to all which he answered that he wondered they would
not be satisfied with so many answers that he had sent, "and desired
them to be assured that he would not go out of the Castle till the
King sent him order so to do." Offended with these high answers,
they resolved to assault it.'—*Clar. Hist.*, iv. 590.

² See note to page 138.

³ A culverin ball weighed 17½ lbs. A chain shot is to be seen at
Donnington Castle, which would be the sort of projectile used to cut
down a flagstaff.

The flag that so boldly flew for the crown—
With the lion-quarterings[1] circled down!
The standard was gone—and, to hail its removal
Ten[2] thousand men gave a roar of approval.

XXVIII

The halyards were cut in twain!
'Though the flag be down,' said Dare-devil Will,
  'It shall soon be hoist again.
'Full oft from the top of a Maypole high
'I have picked the garland cleverly;
  'Ten years ago at your wedding, Sir John,
  'You may remember how well it was done.
'Though not so young I am active still;
  'I will reeve the halyards again or die!'

XXIX

Dare-devil Will was as good as his word,
He flung down helmet, cuirass, and sword;
And, though the grenadoes[3] around him roared,
To the top of the flagstaff he climbed with the cord,
While comrades applauded the act so brave,
And again aloft did the standard wave.

[1] The Royal Standard of that day was the same as it is now.
[2] The forces of the Parliament drawn up before the Castle are here understated.
[3] Shells. *Grenadoe* is derived from the Spanish for pomegranate. The pomegranate appears very prominently in the ornamental stucco-work of the Alhambra of Granada.

XXX

Said Boys, ' To return their salute 'tis fair,
' So point me our culverin all in the air;
' You may give them a dozen [1] degrees at least.
' Give fire !' he cried when the pointing ceased :
Then from the walls burst a salvo loud,
And the balls flew forth of a wreathèd cloud,
Bounding as far as the troops on the plain,
While the houses of Newbury rattled again.

XXXI

' Charge [2] again, but reserve your fire ! '
Said Colonel Boys, who effect did admire,
For stir in the enemy's ranks was seen,
With horse in confusion and wigs on the green.

XXXII

The haughty Ireton was filled with choler,
Manchester blessed (!) them, and so did Waller ·
And ' a forlorn ' to the front they form
With a most wicked intent to storm ;
Four hundred men they have chosen with care,
Fellows all prompt to do and to dare,
And a mighty faggot [3] hath each man there
   As a shield—and a preparation

[1] *Ricochet* fire was not employed generally until after this period.
[2] In the sense of ' load.'
[3] A fascine, or large bundle of sticks.

For filling the fosse[1]
That the rest may cross,
And to light up a conflagration.
Grenadoes[2] good store all ready to fling, with them
Forward they carry
The place to harry;[3]
And thirty-five twenty-foot ladders they bring with
them.
All are with zeal and ardour elate
(The relief behind them is three times as great).
With consolation by preachers supplied;
And with hot strong[4] waters fortified,
' Down with malignants!' they lustily cried.

XXXIII

' To march ' then Ireton giveth the word,
And bids them ' fall on, in the name of the Lord,
' And put ev'ry man in the place to the sword!'[5]

XXXIV

Think you I mock at the Puritan men?
Friends, if you do, you mistake me, then.

---

[1] Ditch of the Castle.

[2] In this instance *hand-grenades* are meant.

[3] To annoy, or harass. 'I will *harry* them out of the land.'—
King James, The Conference at Hampton Court.

[4] The author of the *Story of Corfe Castle*, amongst other items in
the accounts of the Committee of Dorset County for 1643, when
Corfe Castle was assaulted by Parliament troops, quotes the following:—' Aug. 2. For a firkin of hot waters for the soldiers when
they scaled the Castle, 1*l.* 12*s.*'—*Story of Corfe Castle,* p. 313.

[5] The advance of this ' forlorn ' must have presented something of
the appearance of Birnam wood on the march.

Though I love not firebrands, religious or civil,
Or those who the throne and the altar would level—
Though I hate THE CAUSE[1] as I hate the Devil—
The man who risks body and bones i' the fight
For what *I* think wrong, but what *he* thinks right,
My respect shall have, not my scorn or slight.
But worse than cockatrice, vulture, or kite,
Is he who in pulpit makes it his mission
With Gospel trumpet to blow up sedition,[2]
Or by canting[3] speech on the Parliament floor
Makes or prolongs an unnatural war.
Friends!—he that useth religion as ladder
   To rise, in the midst of a nation's ferment,
   To some high post or place of preferment,
Deserves to be dealt with as poisonous adder;
Beware of his head—for with venom 'tis filled,
But let him be scourged at the tail till he's killed!

XXXV

Vipers accurst!—you have cost us dear,
   For you have undone the nation
By making THE FIEND REBELLION appear
   As THE ANGEL OF REFORMATION![4]

[1] The 'Covenant' Cause.

[2] See *Walker's Sufferings of the Clergy*, under the heading of *Factious Lecturers*, Part I. p. 17.

[3] This word, according to Roger L'Estrange, is derived from the name of a Covenanting preacher named Andrew Cant. He is mentioned in *Baillie's Letters*.

[4] This was a saying of Charles I.—Vide *Seward's Anecdotes*, art. 'Charles I.'

You forge the guns and the balls make hot,
But ever keep well out of reach of the shot;
While to slaughter-house shambles, and charnel-
　　house bed
The poor honest knave goeth bravely instead!

XXXVI

When the 'forlorn' got a nearer view
　　(Which Ireton had ordered to 'march,' as I said),
And saw how much battered were rampart and wall,
They burst forth all in a wild halloo—
Nothing did show which could heart appall;
Donnington seemed quite an easy prey
(The frames of the windows were all shot away,
And the gaps filled with sand-bags and trusses of hay),
And they made quite sure that the place would fall,
Though the royal standard did fly over all.

XXXVII

To a storm-tossed galleon, when waves run high,
Or to wither'd oak while the storm roars by,
Or to grey old lion that's wounded sore,
This shot-wreck'd castle resemblance bore.

XXXVIII

But the storm-tossed ship may an harbour find,
And the old oak brave all the force of the wind,
And of wounded lion you'd best beware,
For his claws are sharp and his teeth can tear!

XXXIX

The chargers were champing their bits in the stall—
Under Dare-devil [1] Will's command,
Beside them all ready to mount did stand
Dragooner and ca-ra-bineer.[2]
Though now but a score [3] they did number in all,
The sight of those troopers could Roundheads appall,
For their sallies had cost them dear.
Hal [4] of the Globe had a party select
The sconce of the sallyport bridge to protect,
And under a wall where no enemy saw them
Humphrey the Can-clinker [5] chief cannoneer [6]
Had a couple of drakes [7] and drag-ropes to draw them,

---

[1] The original commander of the horse had been killed. His name was (Captain) Taylor.

[2] *Sic* in the King's *Articles of War.* Oxford: 1643.

[3] 'Twenty-five horse' were in garrison on October 21, 1644, we gather from *Symonds' Diary*, p. 142.

[4] Theatres were suppressed by the 'godly' party, and actors, being 'disestablished' and persecuted, naturally took the Royal side. If caught playing, they were flogged. Sad to reflect that had Shakespeare survived twenty-eight years or so, he might have felt the 'whips and scorns o' the time' with the rest!

[5]   'And let me the cannakin clink, clink, clink;
         And let me the cannakin clink.'—*Othello.*
But we have it from the best authority that Humphrey did *not* 'put an enemy into his mouth to *steal away his brains.*'

[6] Commanding the artillery.

[7] Drakes were used as 'light' field artillery.

With twenty mattrosses[1] and fireworkers[2] ten ;
Their matches alight had the linstock[3] men.

XL

Boys had been up on the barbican[4] tow'r,
  But now he came clattering down the stair,
For he saw the approach of the Parliament pow'r,
    And that while sundry feints south and east they
      prepare,
        Their forlorn did advance from the north.
At the Governor's word ev'ry Royalist man
    Did unto his post go forth.
But most to the sallyport bastion ran,
  Crouching full low so as not to be seen ;
    So runneth the game-bird by hedges of green
      Which of birding-piece[5] is aware.

XLI

' Down under cover, my merry men all ! '
Boys had called out from the top of the wall ;
· Each one his duty doth perfectly know,
  ' But move not a finger till I give the word
' To spring up together and fire on the foe,
  ' And let not a sound be heard ! '

---

[1] Men who helped the gunner to work the guns.
[2] Men who had gone through a laboratory course.
[3] The linstock man was an ancient institution. He is still preserved at Gibraltar and other places.
[4] The Gate-house Tower, which is still in existence.
[5] Fowling-piece.

XLII

Shortly resounded the thundering tread
    Of four hundred stalwart men,
But the garrison seemeth asleep or dead,
      While into the fosse
      Their faggots they toss—
For nothing was seen, and no word was said,
Except that old Robin [1] cried ' Bring up your lead [2]
' And your pitch to pour down on the enemy's head,'
And also there sounded a lumbering din
Like to running up falcon and culverin.

[1] The Quartermaster and Lucy's uncle.

[2] Molten lead was, of course, freely used by both Cavaliers and Parliamentarians in house defence. The following curious account shows how it was successfully employed by the latter :—

The County Messenger (Parliament side), October 4 to 14, 1644.— ' A garrison of ours, ... a house belonging to Mr. Milburn, ... where were forty of our foot soldiers and two small troops, both consisting of but sixty horse, with whom powder and shot being scant, a maide of the house brought them a bag full of six pound weight, and supplied our men with lead out of the glass windows and molten pewter, with which, together with stones out of the house and scalding water, they kept the enemy off until we came to relieve them. Then we fell upon them, killed many of them, and pursued the rest three miles. I never saw (saith the writer) tho sword cut and destroy so many. The Welsh rogues burnt two ricks of Mr. Milburn's corn. Our Governor' (of Monmouth) 'gave the maide two pieces for her powder, and hath taken her into his service; he also kissed her for the good service she did, and so did all the rest of the commanders.'

XLIII

Two hundred of those brave Puritan men
　　Into the fosse their faggots had thrown,
And ladders were sliding in, nine or ten,
When the cocking of matches[1] did faintly sound,
As a cautioning whisper from Boys went round
　　　To pour in the hailstorm dire;
　　　　And his merry men all
　　　　Rose up at his call—
　　' Make ready!—present!—give fire!'[2]

XLIV

And loud did the Royalists shout from the wall,
For at least threescore of their foes did fall!

XLV

You may readily guess, the 'forlorn' looked aghast,
They dropped their grenadoes and faggots in haste,
　　　And staggering back withdrew,
While the gunners above plied their canister[3] fast
　　　As they had been order'd to do.

---

[1] *I.e.*, matchlocks.

[2] The authorised word of command at this time.

[3] Canister (or case) was constantly used in the Civil War. Mr. Hunt, who farmed Donnington Castle, found in the grounds near the wall of the Castle the remains of one of those which undoubtedly had belonged to the magazine of Sir John Boys.

XLVI

Then Boys shouted—' Down with the Covenant carles !'[1]
And his merry men answer'd with—' Hey ! for King
    Charles ! '
The relief to the parapet came,
And eager as hunter to follow the game,
Dare-devil Will and the horse clatter'd out,
And Humphrey and drakes followed hard in his route ;
And seizing a banner, the Governor then
Through the sallyport ran at the head of his men,
While over their heads the grenadoe and ball
    Went whizzing, and roaring, and thundering down
From all the great guns upon Donnington wall,
    While windows did rattle in Newbury town ![2]

XLVII

As he saw what befell, thus did Manchester say :—
' The hand of the Lord is full heavy this day !
' General Cromwell, your horse you must bring
    ' Or triumph the Royalist wins ! '
But Cromwell he little did relish the thing :
    ' No service, my lord,
    ' Shall your horse here afford.'

[1] ' Carle' is a Scotch word, but the Governor was of course think-
ing of the Scottish pedigree of ' The Covenant.'

[2] In this passage and others the resources of the little garrison
in artillery are much exaggerated. *Symonds*, in his *Diary*, before
quoted from, states that Colonel Boys had only 'four pieces of
cannon.' It must, however, be remembered that he also had all the
King's heaviest 'ordnance' under his care. See footnote, *ante*, p. 147.

And Cromwell then added the insolent word,
' Your lordship can take their skins.' [1]

XLVIII

' Hazelrigg, take ye your "lobsters" [2] and go;
' Punish this daring papistical [3] foe.'
But Hazelrigg also to move was slow,
And the shot kept falling so fast and near
That Manchester threw his whole line to the rear.

XLIX

Boys moved direct at the Puritan ranks,
While Dare-devil Will harassed boldly their flanks,
And Humphrey the Can-clinker, playing of pranks,
    And dragging his drakes through the mud and
        the mire,
    Did frequently pour in a flanking fire.

---

[1] This speech was really Cromwell's, though not made till about
a week after this. It is remarkable, however, that the renowned
' ironsides ' and ' lobsters ' achieved so little in the attacks on this
little Castle. The sorties of Boys and his men, especially on this
occasion, were crowned with success. It seems not improbable that
Cromwell, Hazelrigg, and Balfour declined to risk their credit on
any serious attempt to support the assaulting party.

[2] Sir Arthur Hazelrigg's regiment, called *lobsters*, from being
encased in steel from crown to heel. Their ' steel suits ' were
painted red.—*Clar. Hist.*, iv. 460. See also *History of British
Army*, by Sir Sibbald Scott.

[3] The Cavaliers, from the King and Laud downwards, generally
were accused of being ' Papists.'

L

' At them, my merry men !—charge !—for the King !'
Boys to his party did cheerily sing;
For the Parliament colonel did rally his men,
And brought them all up in good order again.

LI

At ' push of pike ' and at ' dint of sword '[1]
The Roundhead and Royalist met at the word.

LII

' Thou bloody malignant !—have at thee then !'
Cried the Parliament chief the attack who led,
And he sprang at Sir John as the challenge he made.
  Stout of limb
  Was that Puritan grim,
And an iron-worker[2] he was by trade ;
A halbert he swung, and a swashing[3] blow
  Discharging with fury on Boys his head,

[1] For these terms see the King's *Articles of War*, Oxford, 1643.

[2] See *Buckle's History of Civilisation*, i. 601, *et seq.*, to show that *all the distinguished officers* of the Parliament army were mechanics and tradesmen, &c. Col. Jones, a serving man ; Venner, a wine cooper ; Whalley, a draper's apprentice ; Berkstead, a pedlar ; Downing, a poor charity boy ; Rolfe, a shoemaker ; Hewson, a cobbler ; Fox, a tinker, &c.

For an account of the fortunes these and their peers accumulated, see *Mystery of the Two Junctos.*

[3] ' Gregory—remember thy *swashing* blow.'—*Romeo and Juliet*, act i. sc. 1.

Down in the dust he has laid him low !
'Hurrah ! hurrah !' cried the jubilant foe.
But Boys again on his feet did stand,
And the staff of the banner he held in his hand
At his opponent he levelleth straight,
And into his forehead he dash'd its weight !

LIII

Then, like an ox that is fell'd in the stall
Dead, that brave Round-headed colonel did fall;
   And away all his force did fly,
    And the Royalists there
    All at once rent the air
   With a cheer for their victory !
And sent a last volley the vanquish'd to gall;
While comrades within and the wounded men all
Cried, ' GOD SAVE KING CHARLES !' upon Donnington[1]
wall !

[1] 'With the very mention of these places,' says the Earl of Car-
narvon, 'how many of the great actors seem to rise and pass across
the theatre of our county history! * * * There we recognise
Sir John Boys with his laconic messages, and his vigorous measures,
vowing that he will hold out Donnington Castle while one stone but
stands above the other, laughing at the fiction—and a monstrous
fiction it was—of fighting for the King against his armies, and doing
his duty cheerfully, fearlessly, and successfully against all odds.'—
The Archæology of Berks (J. Murray), 1859. 'A grand and chival-
rous soldier was Boys,' remarks the *Quarterly Review*, July 1859,
'worthy to be remembered in Berkshire and elsewhere as an example
of that unflinching heroism to which every Englishman should attune
his mind.'

STAVE THE FOURTEENTH.

Castle and Cavalier Triumphant.

N

STAVE THE FOURTEENTH.

Castle and Cavalier triumphant.

I

To celebrate the achievement won,
Of pikes they form a triumphal throne,
And on to their shoulders they hoist Sir John.
The Parliament army all heard the din
That did sound from the hill as they carried him in.

II

But Boys touched Dare-devil Will by the hand,
And stammer'd, ‘I do not this well understand—
‘Something hath happen'd to me I fear—
‘Let Robert of Farningham[1] take the command.’

III

Then pausing, he said, with an utterance clear,
‘A carrier-pigeon to Oxford let fly
‘And let the King know of our victory;

[1] Q. Robert Stradlyn?   See Certificates of, State Papers, July, 1660.

N 2

' And add, while the pray'r[1] for relief you repeat—
' *Except the troop-horses, we've nothing to eat.*

IV

' To my four little wenches[2] then please you to write—
" If leave from the King I may chance to obtain
" I hope during winter to see them again."
' To Merton Street, Oxford, the letter indite.'

V

And then something wildly Sir John did stare,
    And said, ' My bold defiance bear
        ' Unto Nathaniel Finch,
    ' For he who rivalry will dare
        ' Must not from combat flinch.
' But, Will, you must tell her, whate'er may befall,
' I come at my fairest Elizabeth's call
' To join in the carol, and feast in the hall.
    ' Ah, well doth the lovely Elizabeth sing ! '

[1] Dare-devil Will probably remembered that the King could not
return to Oxford from Bath before three or four days had elapsed. A
letter in the terms as above was sent on October 31. See digest of
it in *Warburton's Prince Rupert and the Cavaliers.* It is addressed
to Nicholas.

[2] Jane, Elizabeth, Lucy, and Anne. Jane, the eldest, was at this
time about eight years old. Boys seems to have had a partiality for
the name of Elizabeth. His first child, who died in infancy, bore
that name.

VI

Dare-devil Will with anxiety heard,
For he knew by that incoherent word
  That the Governor's mind it was wandering!

VII

For a terrible blow had that Puritan giv'n
Ere Boys had despatch'd his soul to heav'n.

VIII

And puzzled thought and fever'd brain
Were turning to the past again,
And Mem'ry from her treasure-store
Brought up events of days of yore
And things of ten years past or more;
And, ah, how many joys and fears
Are lost in half a score of years!

IX

Nathaniel Finch in marble sleeps,
  His effigy is sculptured fair,
A bright stone angel o'er him weeps,
  His hands point upwards as in pray'r,
In ruff and jerkin doth he lie
Beneath his high white canopy.
  Of late—despite his widow's care—
Some, who at superstition scoff,
      What art had graced
      Have sore defaced,

And the pale hands have splintered off.
The poor shall long lament in vain
That gen'rous Christian gentleman—
Yet not in vain, for pray'rs and sighs
Of grateful humble folks may rise,
Perchance, like incense to the skies.

X

Elizabeth, his only heir,
Of his estate gets little share,
Of that the Derby-house[1] take care,
For those who to the King are true
Are robb'd of all by Roundhead crew;
Full oft they fleeced Nathaniel Finch,
And now his widow they will pinch.[2]

XI

And gentle-hearted Lucy sleeps—
No marble angel o'er her weeps—
   Her little daughters decked with flow'rs
The mound of green in old churchyard,
Which now they can no longer guard,
   Because the high usurping pow'rs
Have driv'n their father forth to fight
For Church and laws and kingdom's right.

[1] The committee of both kingdoms.
[2] A brief inspection of Royalist composition papers in the Record Office will show how the widows and orphans of Royalists were treated in those terrible times.

XII

When loyal men were hunted down
By the schismatic Parliament,
And Rebel hands
Seized house[1] and lands,
They left the pleasant fields of Kent,
And refuge took in Oxford town.
In weary march they bore their part,
And rode upon a baggage-cart.
The father stay'd[2] at Donnington,
But all his little ones went on—
Their hearts were sad—
Some viands in a wallet stowed,
A fragment of a chain of gold,
Jacobus[3] in an apron sewed,
A portrait of a palfrey white,
From frame cut off and tightly roll'd—
Was almost all the wealth they had.

XIII

An attic[4] by a friend prepared
Received each pallid little guest,

[1] Bonnington, the estate of Sir John Boys, was of course seized and sequestrated, like the estates of all those who took the King's side.

[2] As before mentioned, Colonel Boys assumed the Governorship of Donnington Castle late in the autumn of 1643.

[3] A broad piece (gold) of James I.

[4] At this time Oxford was the refuge of the families of those Royalists who, with the King, shared the toils and perils of the campaign. While the triumphing ' Parliament' men made havoc of

Their frugal supper when they'd shar'd,
    They all prepared to go to rest;
And shiv'ring—for 'twas autumn then,
    And down the dark street howled the wind—
They prayed that peace might come again,
    And that their Maker, good and kind,
Would father ' help to watch and ward
' In the tall house above the trees,
        ' And also guard
        ' In old churchyard
' The flow'rs that grew on grassy mound,
' Till Daisy and mamma were found.'
    And then they rose from off their knees;
And when they all were warm in bed,
    The pretty little Lucy said,
' When good King Charles in peace shall reign,
    ' And this Rebellion is put down,
' Mamma on Daisy shall again
        ' Come riding into Oxford town!'

XIV

The carrier-dove to Oxford flies,
Full soon King Charles the triumph knew;
A letter reached the children too.

XV

But their father, the colonel, insensible lies;
And when the word through the castle ran

park and manor house, noble ladies by scores and hundreds, with
their children, were glad to find shelter in the back streets and lanes
of the loyal city.—See *Catherine Fanshawe's Account.*

That the leech did deem him a dying man,
There was scarce one of his bold cavaliers
Whose eyes did not presently [1] fill up with tears.

XVI

But helpless there while the Governor lay
A nurse did watch him by night and by day;
And she the chirurgeon did something defy,
For failed had Hippocrates' remedy,
And he quoted Galen to prove he should die.

XVII

The garrison starving, the Governor dying!
It is a sad and desperate case.
Colonel Sir John on his back is lying!
But there the nurse still sat in her place.

XVIII

Sev'n days have past since his hurt was done,
And they said, 'With the leaf he shall fade and fall;
'His race is ended, his sand is run!'
For there on his bed he lay motionless all,
While the rays of the mild November sun
Fell faint but warm on the chamber wall;
Had the leaves in the park been less yellow and sere,
You might have supposed it the spring of the year.

XIX

Behold!—of a sudden he moves! he sighs!
And then for a moment half opens his eyes;

---

[1] *i.e.* immediately.

And turns on his side,
To open them wide,
And, with a vacant and dreamy stare,
Fixes them on his attendant there,
And muttereth, ' Is it some trick of the brain,
' Or am I once more in old Barham again
' With mine ancient playmate so kind and fair ? '
And as the lov'd face to his memory came
He calleth his darling enchantress by name—
For the Lady Elizabeth Finch was there!

XX

To the starv'd-out castle, where prostrate he lay,
She had made through the lines of the leaguer her way ;
'Twas *she* who had watch'd him by night and by day ;
And, oh ! with what joy fair Elizabeth learns
By that half-mutter'd speech that his reason returns !

XXI

' 'Tis thine old playmate who sits by thy side—
' But speak not, dear John, for the present,' she cried.

XXII

Then the lovely Elizabeth up did stand,
For Boys did right eagerly stretch forth his hand,
Which she to her tender sweet bosom did press,
And bent o'er her true-love with gentle caress ;
While tears on the coverlet fast did fall
As she thought how they parted in Kentish Hall!

XXIII

Then sudden there came a cry!—
'Huzza! huzza!'—from the top of the wall,
In chorus full loud—for his merry men all
    Did His Majesty's army espy—
And trumpet and kettle-drum, echoing far,
Sound faintly where Boys and Elizabeth are;
    And again pealed that chorus high,
For well you may guess that those hunger-pinch'd men
Rejoiced for to see the King's[1] banner again.

XXIV

Prince Rupert and horse come the convoy before;
The *sight* of the flour-sacks and wagons, good store,
    And muttons and beeves[2]
    Half their hunger relieves,
All fear of their yielding thro' famine is o'er.

XXV

Over the river Prince Rupert will go
    (And the same is approv'd by the King),
    A challenge of present[3] defiance to fling
In the face of the Parliament foe.
But first those supplies, all the hungry to fill,
Are drawn and are driven up Donnington hill.

[1] The King's army arrived at Donnington Castle on November 9th, 1644 (at about 1 o'clock), and relieved it.
[2] Live stock—sheep and oxen.
[3] *i.e.* instant.

XXVI

Full loud was the clatter in Newbury town,
  With horse and with train-bands all running to arms,
  The Parliamentarians it something alarms
To hear of the King coming suddenly down.

XXVII

Down by the castle King Charles doth go,
  Over the fords of the Lamborne river;
While kettle-drums beat and the trumpets blow,
And the old oaks ring to the clamour below—
  The like again it shall happen there never.[1]
So long was that brilliant and gay cavalcade,
Two hours were consumed while the crossing was
  made.

XXVIII

Bright were the breast-plates and head-pieces there,
        And buff-suits laced
        Half the Cavaliers graced,
And scarfs of silk tissue those gallants did wear.
They follow the course of the Lamborne down,
And flaunt all their banners in sight of the town;
The Roundheaded men may come on if they choose,
The Royalists will not the combat refuse.

---

[1] This was nearly the last *bravado* of the King's army. On June
14th following was fought the fatal battle of Naseby, which destroyed
at once the power and hopes of the Royalists.

XXIX

My friends, I will not the adage here quote,
Which tells what may happen when rogues fall out,
But since the assault of the castle did fail
The Roundheads have been at it tooth and nail.
Such strife did that day in their councils prevail
That though in Battalia, 'twixt Speen and the town,
The Royalists stood—yet the foe came not on;
And tho' the King's army march'd nearly to Shaw,
But little of Parliament valour they saw.[1]

[1] ' The King met Prince Rupert, as he expected, with Colonel Ger-
rard and Sir Marmaduke Langdale, and made all the haste he could
to join those forces with his own army, that so he might march back
to Newbury and disengage his cannon and carriages. By the way
he met the Earl of Northampton and those regiments which had
relieved Banbury, and having with marvellous expedition caused a
new train of artillery to be formed, he brought his army to ren-
dezvous on Bullington Green, where, with the addition of some foot
which he drew out of Oxford, under the command of Colonel Gage,
it appeared to be full 6,000 foot and 5,000 horse, with which he
marched to Wallingford; and within a day more than a week after
he had left Donnington Castle, found himself there again in so good
a posture that he resolved not to decline fighting with the enemy;
but would first be possessed of his cannon and put some provision
into the Castle; which he accomplished without any opposition.
' The enemy's army lay still at Newbury, perplexed with the divisions and factions among their own officers, without any notice of
the King's advance till a quarter of their horse was beaten up. . . . .
The King's army . . . . marched by the Castle over the river by
a mill and two fords below it, without any opposition, and thence
drew into the large field between Speen and Newbury, which was
thought a good place to expect the enemy, who in the meantime had

XXX

At the close of that still November day—
  Which some St. Martin's summer did call—
All the King's host with Prince Rupert lay
  In the ancient park under Donnington wall;
Soon by the golden light of the stars
Was fixed the camp of those sons of Mars.

XXXI

And they treated their comrades of Donnington there,
  Quaffing and roaring forth Royalist lays

drawn a great body of their horse and foot into the other field
towards Shaw, and had made breastworks and batteries on the back
side of Newbury, which town they resolved to keep, and stand
upon the defensive, as the King had done before; presuming that
they, now having the warmer lodging, might better attack the King
after his men had lain a night or two in the fields, it being now the
month of November, *but fair for that season.* Some light skir-
mishes past between the horse; but when the King saw upon what
disadvantages he must force them to fight, he called his council
together, who were unanimous in opinion " that since he had relieved
the Castle, and put sufficient provisions into it, and that it was in
his power to draw off his ordnance and ammunition from thence, he
had done his business; and if any honour had been lost the other
day " (October 27), " it was regained now, by his having passed his
army over the river in the face of theirs and offered them battle,
which they durst not accept."

'Upon which the King resolved to attempt them no farther, but
gave orders to retire in their view, with drums beating and trumpets
sounding, the same way he came over the river. So the King lay
that night at Donnington Castle, and all the army about him.'—
Clar. Hist., iv. 590.

With such as were willing their mirth to share ;
While their umber'd faces did front the blaze
Of the fires that did send up their wreaths of smoke
Round 'the King's,'[1] and 'the Queen's,' and old
' Chaucer's ' oak.

XXXII

His Majesty did not those revels attend,
But by the bedside of his servant and friend
Talking he sat, and his state did unbend
    To the Governor and to that nurse so fair,
And told of his hope that the war would end ;[2]
    While through shatter'd casement did float the air
And the light of the bivouac bonfires shone ;
        And from time to time
        They did list to the chime
Of those Royalist songs—and here followeth one
    Which the King did that night commend :
And I'd have you to know that his Majesty's praise[3]
Is never at random bestowed upon lays :—

[1] It is to be inferred from *Evelyn* (see note, *ante*, p. 138) that
these celebrated oaks were standing at this period.

[2] About this time the abortive Treaty of Uxbridge was projected.
In spite of what has been maliciously asserted to the contrary, the
King, who did not begin the war, was ever desirous of concluding
peace.

[3] King Charles I., whose taste and knowledge of high art in all
its branches is well known, and who was so clever with his hands
that he used to boast there was scarce any mechanical trade that he
could not have made a livelihood by working at, was a composer of
songs and anthems.

All is fair in Love and War.

1

The Royal arms the banner bore,
Her own dear hand had 'broider'd o'er;
So lovely and so true was she,
He swore her faithful knight to be,
Forsaking all he priz'd before—
For all is fair in love and war!

2

Said he, ' From those bright eyes I learn
' How Roundheads Cavaliers may turn;
' Aside my steeple-hat I'll fling,
' And draw the sword for Church and King;
' The Cov'nant vow I'll keep no more—
' For all is fair in love and war!'

3

The father scorn'd the knight so brave,
The daughter's hand the banner gave—
The ' faithful city' heard the call—
He waved it high on Worcester wall,
And off the lovely bride he bore—
For all is fair in love and war!

All is fair in Love and War.

Allegro.

The Roy - al Arms the Ban - ner bore, Her own dear hand had 'broi - der'd o'er ; So love - ly and so true was she, He swore her faith - ful knight to be, For - sa - king all he priz'd be - fore, For all is fair in Love and War, For all is fair, for all is fair, for all is fair in Love and War. For all is fair, for all is fair, for all is fair in Love and War!

rall

tempo.

CHORUS.

rall

O

XXXIII

There was a strain in that loyal air
That did touch the hearts of that noble pair.

XXXIV

The standard that flew on the castle wall
Had not been wrought by Elizabeth's hand;
But for Church and Crown she had taken her stand,
    And she scorned the Rebels both great and small,
And honoured the man who their might defied
And had drawn his sword for the weaker side.

XXXV

And while the words and the measure did rise,
    The King, who hath observation keen,
    Glancing at Boys and his fancy's queen,
Saw that their souls did unite through their eyes;
But to feelings strong and tender and true
His Majesty knows the respect that is due.

XXXVI

When the sun was chasing the frost-fog gray
    From Snelsmore Heath on the tenth of November
All the King's army are marching away;
    And Noll and Manchester both may remember
How bold Prince Rupert, before they were gone,
Sent[1] a trumpet 'to know if they'd please to fall on?'

---

[1] This circumstance is chronicled by a Royalist diurnal.

XXXVII

Boys would not have his belovèd to stay
 In that dangerous shot-wreck'd tow'r;
  He said her ' nay '
  When she prayed to remain,
 And swore that he felt himself well again.
  So, safe from the Rebels' pow'r,
 To Oxford she goes in his Majesty's care,
To watch o'er his four little daughters so fair.

XXXVIII

The wheels of Time they go rolling on—
The foe into winter quarters is gone;
Musket and partisan, pike and spear,
Come no longer the castle so near.

XXXIX

Keeping well clear of great Wood-monger[1] Brown,
Boys he is riding tow'rds Oxford town;
Afar the tow'rs and the steeples gray
Did coldly glimmer on Christmas-day,
 While the snow-show'r thin did fall;
He buried his chin in his mantle's fold,
And thought of his rides unto Barham of old.

[1] General Brown, the ' fagot-seller,' Governor of Abingdon for the Parliament. Abingdon is between Newbury and Oxford. Sir John would be obliged to go by way of Wallingford.

XL

At ten of the clock he approached the wall ;
  The word is passed—he has giv'n his name ;
  All had heard of his deeds of fame,
And down the High Street the word did run—
' Here comes the defender of Donnington ! '

XLI

An usher the King had sent,
  And a handsome coach of state ;
  His four little daughters got in at the gate,
A guard rode beside them, and forward they went.

XLII

In spite of the cold, each casement wide
Was open'd, as down the street they did ride,
  While troopers in buff full loud did roar,
  And the crowd their volleys of cheers did pour,
And dames and maidens of high degree
    Their kerchiefs did wave
    For that knight so brave,
Who had serv'd the King with such loyalty ;
  Sir John the ovation quietly bore.

XLIII

The King was waiting in Christ-Church hall,
On the daïs he stood with his courtiers all ;

The hall it was gaily decked with green,
And holly and ivy did grace the scene,
With mistletoe hanging the rafters between;
For it needs not to loyal men *here* be told
    (Though a crime by the Roundheads made it hath
      been)
That the King is a lover of customs old.

XLIV

Sir John he knelt to His Majesty there,
   And he pressed his lady-love dear, to his heart.
You may be sure that Elizabeth fair
Was safe from harm in His Majesty's care;
   And from Boys she never again will part.

XLV

A bridal feast they do straight prepare;
King Charles the lady away he gave;
Hyde and Southampton, and Capel so brave—
   His Highness Prince Rupert too—
Richmond and Hertford, and nobles a score—
Time it would take for to reckon them o'er—
With many a lady, as I could tell,
Did greet the lovers and wish them well;
   And to cheer their hearts so true,
The high bells of Christ Church did merrily ring!

My friends, I have no more to say or to sing.
I pray you your caps i' the air all to fling,
While low on the knee I do pledge you—THE KING!

Vivat in æternum Rex Carolus!

THE END.

LONDON PRINTED BY
SPOTTISWOODE AND CO., NEW-STREET SQUARE
AND PARLIAMENT STREET

GENERAL LIST OF WORKS

PUBLISHED BY

MESSRS. LONGMANS, GREEN, AND CO.

PATERNOSTER ROW, LONDON.

History, Politics, Historical Memoirs, &c.

The **HISTORY** of **ENGLAND** from the Fall of Wolsey to the Defeat of the Spanish Armada. By JAMES ANTHONY FROUDE, M.A. late Fellow of Exeter College, Oxford.
> LIBRARY EDITION, 12 VOLS. 8vo. price £8 18s.
> CABINET EDITION, in 12 vols. crown 8vo. price 72s.

The **HISTORY** of **ENGLAND** from the Accession of James II. By Lord MACAULAY.
> STUDENT'S EDITION, 2 vols. crown 8vo. 12s.
> PEOPLE'S EDITION, 4 vols. crown 8vo. 16s.
> CABINET EDITION, 8 vols. post 8vo. 48s.
> LIBRARY EDITION, 5 vols. 8vo. £4.

LORD MACAULAY'S WORKS. Complete and Uniform Library Edition. Edited by his Sister, Lady TREVELYAN. 8 vols. 8vo. with Portrait, price £5 5s. cloth, or £8 8s. bound in tree-calf by Rivière.

VARIETIES of **VICE-REGAL LIFE.** By Sir WILLIAM DENISON, K.C.B. late Governor-General of the Australian Colonies, and Governor of Madras. With Two Maps. 2 vols. 8vo. 28s.

On **PARLIAMENTARY GOVERNMENT** in **ENGLAND**: Its Origin, Development, and Practical Operation. By ALPHEUS TODD, Librarian of the Legislative Assembly of Canada. 2 vols. 8vo. price £1 17s.

A **HISTORICAL ACCOUNT** of the **NEUTRALITY** of **GREAT BRITAIN DURING** the AMERICAN CIVIL WAR. By MOUNTAGUE BERNARD, M.A. Chichele Professor of International Law and Diplomacy in the University of Oxford. Royal 8vo. 16s.

The **CONSTITUTIONAL HISTORY** of **ENGLAND**, since the Accession of George III. 1760—1860. By Sir THOMAS ERSKINE MAY, C.B. Second Edition. Cabinet Edition, thoroughly revised. 3 vols. crown 8vo. price 18s.

The **HISTORY** of **ENGLAND**, from the Earliest Times to the Year 1865. By C. D. YONGE, Regius Professor of Modern History in Queen's College, Belfast. New Edition. Crown 8vo. price 7s. 6d.

A

The OXFORD REFORMERS—John Colet, Erasmus, and Thomas More; being a History of their Fellow-work. By FREDERIC SEEBOHM. Second Edition, enlarged. 8vo. 14s.

LECTURES on the HISTORY of ENGLAND, from the earliest Times to the Death of King Edward II. By WILLIAM LONGMAN. With Maps and Illustrations. 8vo. 15s.

The HISTORY of the LIFE and TIMES of EDWARD the THIRD. By WILLIAM LONGMAN. With 9 Maps, 8 Plates, and 16 Woodcuts. 2 vols. 8vo. 28s.

The OVERTHROW of the GERMANIC CONFEDERATION by PRUSSIA in 1866. By Sir ALEXANDER MALET, Bart. K.C.B. With 5 Maps. 8vo. 18s.

The MILITARY RESOURCES of PRUSSIA and FRANCE, and RECENT CHANGES in the ART of WAR. By Lieut.-Col. CHESNEY, R.E. and HENRY REEVE, D.C.L. Crown 8vo. price 7s. 6d.

WATERLOO LECTURES; a Study of the Campaign of 1815. By Colonel CHARLES C. CHESNEY, R.E. late Professor of Military Art and History in the Staff College. New Edition. 8vo. with Map, 10s. 6d.

DEMOCRACY in AMERICA. By ALEXIS DE TOCQUEVILLE. Translated by HENRY REEVE. 2 vols. 8vo. 21s.

HISTORY of the REFORMATION in EUROPE in the Time of Calvin. By J. H. MERLE D'AUBIGNÉ, D.D. VOLS. I. and II. 8vo. 28s. VOL. III. 12s. VOL. IV. 16s. VOL. V. price 16s.

CHAPTERS from FRENCH HISTORY; St. Louis, Joan of Arc, Henri IV. with Sketches of the Intermediate Periods. By J. H. GURNEY, M.A. New Edition. Fcp. 8vo. 6s. 6d.

MEMOIR of POPE SIXTUS the FIFTH. By Baron HUBNER. Translated from the Original in French, with the Author's sanction, by HUBERT E. H. JERNINGHAM. 2 vols. 8vo. [*In preparation.*

IGNATIUS LOYOLA and the EARLY JESUITS. By STEWART ROSE. New Edition, revised. 8vo. with Portrait, price 16s.

The HISTORY of GREECE. By C. THIRLWALL, D.D. Lord Bishop of St. David's. 8 vols. fcp. 8vo. price 28s.

GREEK HISTORY from Themistocles to Alexander, in a Series of Lives from Plutarch. Revised and arranged by A. H. CLOUGH. New Edition. Fcp. with 44 Woodcuts, 6s.

CRITICAL HISTORY of the LANGUAGE and LITERATURE of Ancient Greece. By WILLIAM MURE, of Caldwell. 5 vols. 8vo. £3 9s.

The TALE of the GREAT PERSIAN WAR, from the Histories of Herodotus. By GEORGE W. COX, M.A. New Edition. Fcp. 3s. 6d.

HISTORY of the LITERATURE of ANCIENT GREECE. By Professor K. O. MÜLLER. Translated by the Right Hon. Sir GEORGE CORNEWALL LEWIS, Bart. and by J. W. DONALDSON, D.D. 3 vols. 8vo. 21s.

HISTORY of the CITY of ROME from its Foundation to the Sixteenth Century of the Christian Era. By THOMAS H. DYER, LL.D. 8vo. with 2 Maps, 15s.

The HISTORY of ROME. By WILLIAM IHNE. English Edition, translated and revised by the Author. VOLS. I. and II. 8vo. price 30s.

HISTORY of the ROMANS under the EMPIRE. By the Very Rev. C. MERIVALE, D.C.L. Dean of Ely. 8 vols. post 8vo. 48s.

The FALL of the ROMAN REPUBLIC; a Short History of the Last Century of the Commonwealth. By the same Author. 12mo. 7s. 6d.

A STUDENT'S MANUAL of the HISTORY of INDIA, from the Earliest Period to the Present. By Colonel MEADOWS TAYLOR, M.R.A.S. M.R.I.A. Crown 8vo. with Maps, 7s. 6d.

The HISTORY of INDIA, from the Earliest Period to the close of Lord Dalhousie's Administration. By JOHN CLARK MARSHMAN. 3 vols. crown 8vo. 22s. 6d.

INDIAN POLITY: a View of the System of Administration in India. By Lieutenant-Colonel GEORGE CHESNEY, Fellow of the University of Calcutta. New Edition, revised; with Map. 8vo. price 21s.

HOME POLITICS; being a consideration of the Causes of the Growth of Trade in relation to Labour, Pauperism, and Emigration. By DANIEL GRANT. 8vo. 7s.

REALITIES of IRISH LIFE. By W. STEUART TRENCH, Land Agent in Ireland to the Marquess of Lansdowne, the Marquess of Bath, and Lord Digby. Fifth Edition. Crown 8vo. price 6s.

The STUDENT'S MANUAL of the HISTORY of IRELAND. By MARY F. CUSACK, Author of 'The Illustrated History of Ireland, from the Earliest Period to the Year of Catholic Emancipation.' Crown 8vo. price 6s.

CRITICAL and HISTORICAL ESSAYS contributed to the *Edinburgh Review.* By the Right Hon. LORD MACAULAY.

CABINET EDITION, 4 vols. post 8vo. 24s.	LIBRARY EDITION, 3 vols. 8vo. 36s.
PEOPLE'S EDITION, 2 vols. crown 8vo. 8s.	STUDENT'S EDITION, 1 vol. cr. 8vo. 6s.

SAINT-SIMON and SAINT-SIMONISM; a chapter in the History of Socialism in France. By ARTHUR J. BOOTH, M.A. Crown 8vo. price 7s. 6d.

HISTORY of EUROPEAN MORALS, from Augustus to Charlemagne. By W. E. H. LECKY, M.A. Second Edition. 2 vols. 8vo. price 28s.

HISTORY of the RISE and INFLUENCE of the SPIRIT of RATIONALISM in EUROPE. By W. E. H. LECKY, M.A. Cabinet Edition, being the Fourth. 2 vols. crown 8vo. price 16s.

GOD in HISTORY; or, the Progress of Man's Faith in the Moral Order of the World. By Baron BUNSEN. Translated by SUSANNA WINKWORTH; with a Preface by Dean STANLEY. 3 vols. 8vo. price 42s.

The HISTORY of PHILOSOPHY, from Thales to Comte. By GEORGE HENRY LEWES. Fourth Edition. 2 vols. 8vo. 32s.

An HISTORICAL VIEW of LITERATURE and ART in GREAT BRITAIN from the Accession of the House of Hanover to the Reign of Queen Victoria. By J. MURRAY GRAHAM, M.A. 8vo. price 14s.

The MYTHOLOGY of the ARYAN NATIONS. By GEORGE W. Cox, M.A. late Scholar of Trinity College, Oxford, Joint-Editor, with the late Professor Brande, of the Fourth Edition of 'The Dictionary of Science, Literature, and Art,' Author of 'Tales of Ancient Greece,' &c. 2 vols. 8vo. 28s.

HISTORY of CIVILISATION in England and France, Spain and Scotland. By HENRY THOMAS BUCKLE. New Edition of the entire Work with a complete INDEX. 3 vols. crown 8vo. 24s.

HISTORY of the CHRISTIAN CHURCH, from the Ascension of Christ to the Conversion of Constantine. By E. BURTON, D.D. late Prof. of Divinity in the Univ. of Oxford. New Edition. Fcp. 3s. 6d.

SKETCH of the HISTORY of the CHURCH of ENGLAND to the Revolution of 1688. By the Right Rev. T. V. SHORT, D.D. Lord Bishop of St. Asaph. Eighth Edition. Crown 8vo. 7s. 6d.

HISTORY of the EARLY CHURCH, from the First Preaching of the Gospel to the Council of Nicæa. A.D. 325. By ELIZABETH M. SEWELL, Author of 'Amy Herbert.' New Edition, with Questions. Fcp. 4s. 6d.

The ENGLISH REFORMATION. By F. C. MASSINGBERD, M.A. Chancellor of Lincoln and Rector of South Ormsby. Fourth Edition, revised. Fcp. 8vo. 7s. 6d.

MAUNDER'S HISTORICAL TREASURY; comprising a General Introductory Outline of Universal History, and a series of Separate Histories. Latest Edition, revised and brought down to the Present Time by the Rev. GEORGE WILLIAM COX, M.A. Fcp. 6s. cloth, or 9s. 6d. calf.

HISTORICAL and CHRONOLOGICAL ENCYCLOPÆDIA; comprising Chronological Notices of all the Great Events of Universal History: Treaties, Alliances, Wars, Battles, &c.; Incidents in the Lives of Eminent Men and their Works, Scientific and Geographical Discoveries, Mechanical Inventions, and Social, Domestic, and Economical Improvements. By B. B. WOODWARD, B.A. and W. L. R CATES. 1 vol. 8vo.   [*In the press.*

Biographical Works.

A MEMOIR of DANIEL MACLISE, R.A. By W. JUSTIN O'DRISCOLL, M.R.I.A. Barrister-at-Law. With Portrait and Woodcuts. Post 8vo. price 7s. 6d.

MEMOIRS of the MARQUIS of POMBAL; with Extracts from his Writings and from Despatches in the State Papers Office. By the CONDE DA CARNOTA. New Edition. 8vo. price 7s.

REMINISCENCES of FIFTY YEARS. By MARK BOYD. Post 8vo. price 10s. 6d.

The LIFE of ISAMBARD KINGDOM BRUNEL, Civil Engineer. By ISAMBARD BRUNEL, B.C.L. of Lincoln's Inn; Chancellor of the Diocese of Ely. With Portrait, Plates, and Woodcuts. 8vo. 21s.

The LIFE and LETTERS of FARADAY. By Dr. BENCE JONES, Secretary of the Royal Institution. Second Edition, thoroughly revised. 2 vols. 8vo. with Portrait, and Eight Engravings on Wood, price 28s.

FARADAY as a DISCOVERER. By JOHN TYNDALL, LL.D. F.R.S. Professor of Natural Philosophy in the Royal Institution. New and Cheaper Edition, with Two Portraits. Fcp. 8vo. 3s. 6d.

The LIFE and LETTERS of the Rev. SYDNEY SMITH. Edited by his Daughter, Lady HOLLAND, and Mrs. AUSTIN. New Edition, complete in One Volume. Crown 8vo. price 6s.

SOME MEMORIALS of R. D. HAMPDEN, Bishop of Hereford. Edited by his Daughter, HENRIETTA HAMPDEN. With Portrait. 8vo. price 12s.

The **LIFE** and **TRAVELS** of **GEORGE WHITEFIELD, M.A.** By
JAMES PATERSON GLEDSTONE. 8vo. price 14s.

LIVES of the **LORD CHANCELLORS** and **KEEPERS** of the **GREAT**
SEAL of IRELAND, from the Earliest Times to the Reign of Queen
Victoria. By J. R. O'FLANAGAN, M.R.I.A. Barrister-at-Law. 2 vols. 8vo. 36s.

DICTIONARY of **GENERAL BIOGRAPHY**; containing Concise
Memoirs and Notices of the most Eminent Persons of all Countries, from
the Earliest Ages to the Present Time. Edited by W. L. R. CATES. 8vo. 21s.

LIVES of the **QUEENS** of **ENGLAND**. By AGNES STRICKLAND.
Library Edition, newly revised; with Portraits of every Queen, Autographs,
and Vignettes. 8 vols. post 8vo. 7s. 6d. each.

LIFE of the **DUKE** of **WELLINGTON**. By the Rev. G. R. GLEIG,
M.A. Popular Edition, carefully revised; with copious Additions. Crown
8vo. with Portrait, 5s.

HISTORY of **MY RELIGIOUS OPINIONS**. By J. H. NEWMAN, D.D.
Being the Substance of Apologia pro Vitâ Suâ. Post 8vo. 6s.

The **PONTIFICATE** of **PIUS the NINTH**; being the Third Edition
of 'Rome and its Ruler,' continued to the latest moment and greatly
enlarged. By J. F. MAGUIRE, M.P. Post 8vo. with Portrait, 12s. 6d.

FATHER MATHEW: a Biography. By JOHN FRANCIS MAGUIRE,
M.P. for Cork. Popular Edition, with Portrait. Crown 8vo. 3s. 6d.

FELIX MENDELSSOHN'S LETTERS from *Italy and Switzerland*,
and *Letters from* 1833 *to* 1847, translated by Lady WALLACE. New Edition,
with Portrait. 2 vols. crown 8vo. 5s. each.

MEMOIRS of **SIR HENRY HAVELOCK, K.C.B.** By JOHN CLARK
MARSHMAN. Cabinet Edition, with Portrait. Crown 8vo. price 3s. 6d.

VICISSITUDES of **FAMILIES**. By Sir J. BERNARD BURKE, C.B.
Ulster King of Arms. New Edition, remodelled and enlarged. 2 vols.
crown 8vo. 21s.

ESSAYS in **ECCLESIASTICAL BIOGRAPHY**. By the Right Hon.
Sir J. STEPHEN, LL.D. Cabinet Edition, being the Fifth. Crown 8vo. 7s. 6d.

MAUNDER'S BIOGRAPHICAL TREASURY. Thirteenth Edition,
reconstructed, thoroughly revised, and in great part rewritten; with about
1,000 additional Memoirs and Notices, by W. L. R. CATES. Fcp. 6s.

LETTERS and **LIFE** of **FRANCIS BACON**, including all his Occa-
sional Works. Collected and edited, with a Commentary, by J. SPEDDING,
Trin. Coll. Cantab. VOLS. I. and II. 8vo. 24s. VOLS. III. and IV. 24s.
VOL. V. price 12s.

Criticism, Philosophy, Polity, &c.

The **INSTITUTES** of **JUSTINIAN**; with English Introduction, Translation, and Notes. By T. C. SANDARS, M.A. Barrister, late Fellow of Oriel
Coll. Oxon. New Edition. 8vo. 15s.

SOCRATES and the SOCRATIC SCHOOLS. Translated from the German of Dr. E. ZELLER, with the Author's approval, by the Rev. OSWALD J. REICHEL, B.C.L. and M.A. Crown 8vo. 8s. 6d.

The STOICS, EPICUREANS, and SCEPTICS. Translated from the German of Dr. E. ZELLER, with the Author's approval, by OSWALD J. REICHEL, B.C.L. and M.A. Crown 8vo. price 14s.

The ETHICS of ARISTOTLE, illustrated with Essays and Notes. By Sir A. GRANT, Bart. M.A. LL.D. Second Edition, revised and completed. 2 vols. 8vo. price 28s.

The NICOMACHEAN ETHICS of ARISTOTLE newly translated into English. By R. WILLIAMS, B.A. Fellow and late Lecturer of Merton College, and sometime Student of Christ Church, Oxford. 8vo. 12s.

ELEMENTS of LOGIC. By R. WHATELY, D.D. late Archbishop of Dublin. New Edition. 8vo. 10s. 6d. crown 8vo. 4s. 6d.

Elements of Rhetoric. By the same Author. New Edition. 8vo. 10s. 6d. crown 8vo. 4s. 6d.

English Synonymes. By E. JANE WHATELY. Edited by Archbishop WHATELY. 5th Edition. Fcp. 3s.

BACON'S ESSAYS with ANNOTATIONS. By R. WHATELY, D.D. late Archbishop of Dublin. Sixth Edition. 8vo. 10s. 6d.

LORD BACON'S WORKS, collected and edited by J. SPEDDING, M.A. R. L. ELLIS, M.A. and D. D. HEATH. New and Cheaper Edition. 7 vols. 8vo. price £3 13s. 6d.

The SUBJECTION of WOMEN. By JOHN STUART MILL. New Edition. Post 8vo. 5s.

On REPRESENTATIVE GOVERNMENT. By JOHN STUART MILL. Third Edition. 8vo. 9s. Crown 8vo. 2s.

On LIBERTY. By JOHN STUART MILL. Fourth Edition. Post 8vo. 7s. 6d. Crown 8vo. 1s. 4d.

PRINCIPLES of POLITICAL ECONOMY. By the same Author. Eighth Edition. 2 vols. 8vo. 30s. Or in 1 vol. crown 8vo. 5s.

A SYSTEM of LOGIC, RATIOCINATIVE and INDUCTIVE. By the same Author. Seventh Edition. Two vols. 8vo. 25s.

ANALYSIS of Mr. MILL'S SYSTEM of LOGIC. By W. STEBBING, M.A. Fellow of Worcester College, Oxford. New Edition. 12mo. 3s. 6d.

UTILITARIANISM. By JOHN STUART MILL. Fourth Edition. 8vo. 5s.

DISSERTATIONS and DISCUSSIONS, POLITICAL, PHILOSOPHICAL, and HISTORICAL. By JOHN STUART MILL. Second Edition, revised. 3 vols. 8vo. 36s.

EXAMINATION of Sir W. HAMILTON'S PHILOSOPHY, and of the Principal Philosophical Questions discussed in his Writings. By JOHN STUART MILL. Third Edition. 8vo. 16s.

An OUTLINE of the NECESSARY LAWS of THOUGHT: a Treatise on Pure and Applied Logic. By the Most Rev. WILLIAM, Lord Archbishop of York, D.D. F.R.S. Ninth Thousand. Crown 8vo. 5s. 6d.

The **ELEMENTS** of **POLITICAL ECONOMY**. By HENRY DUNNING MACLEOD, M.A. Barrister-at-Law. 8vo. 16s.

A **Dictionary** of **Political Economy**; Biographical, Bibliographical, Historical, and Practical. By the same Author. VOL. I. royal 8vo. 30s.

The **ELECTION** of **REPRESENTATIVES**, Parliamentary and Municipal; a Treatise. By THOMAS HARE, Barrister-at-Law. Third Edition, with Additions. Crown 8vo. 6s.

SPEECHES of the **RIGHT HON. LORD MACAULAY**, corrected by Himself. People's Edition, crown 8vo. 3s. 6d.

Lord Macaulay's Speeches on **Parliamentary Reform** in 1831 and 1832. 16mo. 1s.

INAUGURAL ADDRESS delivered to the University of St. Andrews. By JOHN STUART MILL. 8vo. 5s. People's Edition, crown 8vo. 1s.

A **DICTIONARY** of the **ENGLISH LANGUAGE**. By R. G. LATHAM, M.A. M.D. F.R.S. Founded on the Dictionary of Dr. SAMUEL JOHNSON, as edited by the Rev. H. J. TODD, with numerous Emendations and Additions. In Four Volumes, 4to. price £7.

THESAURUS of **ENGLISH WORDS** and **PHRASES**, classified and arranged so as to facilitate the Expression of Ideas, and assist in Literary Composition. By P. M. ROGET, M.D. New Edition. Crown 8vo. 10s. 6d.

LECTURES on the **SCIENCE** of **LANGUAGE**. By F. MAX MÜLLER, M.A. &c. Foreign Member of the French Institute. Sixth Edition. 2 vols. crown 8vo. price 16s.

CHAPTERS on **LANGUAGE**. By FREDERIC W. FARRAR, F.R.S. Head Master of Marlborough College. Crown 8vo. 8s. 6d.

The **DEBATER**; a Series of Complete Debates, Outlines of Debates, and Questions for Discussion. By F. ROWTON. Fcp. 6s.

MANUAL of **ENGLISH LITERATURE**, Historical and Critical. By THOMAS ARNOLD, M.A. Second Edition. Crown 8vo. price 7s. 6d.

SOUTHEY'S DOCTOR, complete in One Volume. Edited by the Rev. J. W. WARTER, B.D. Square crown 8vo. 12s. 6d.

HISTORICAL and **CRITICAL COMMENTARY** on the **OLD TESTAMENT**; with a New Translation. By M. M. KALISCH, Ph.D. VOL. I. *Genesis*, 8vo. 18s. or adapted for the General Reader, 12s. VOL. II. *Exodus*, 15s. or adapted for the General Reader, 12s. VOL. III. *Leviticus*, PART I. 15s. or adapted for the General Reader, 8s.

A **HEBREW GRAMMAR**, with **EXERCISES**. By M. M. KALISCH, Ph.D. PART I. *Outlines with Exercises*, 8vo. 12s. 6d. KEY, 5s. PART II. *Exceptional Forms and Constructions*, 12s. 6d.

A **LATIN-ENGLISH DICTIONARY**. By JOHN T. WHITE, D.D. Oxon. and J. E. RIDDLE, M.A. Oxon. Third Edition, revised. 2 vols. 4to. pp. 2,128, price 42s. cloth.

White's College Latin-English Dictionary (Intermediate Size), abridged for the use of University Students from the Parent Work (as above). Medium 8vo. pp. 1,048, price 18s. cloth.

White's Junior Student's Complete Latin-English and English-Latin Dictionary. New Edition. Square 12mo. pp. 1,058, price 12s.

Separately { The ENGLISH-LATIN DICTIONARY, price 5s. 6d.
         { The LATIN-ENGLISH DICTIONARY, price 7s. 6d.

An **ENGLISH-GREEK LEXICON**, containing all the Greek Words used by Writers of good authority. By C. D. YONGE, B.A. New Edition. 4to. 21s.

Mr. YONGE'S NEW LEXICON, English and Greek, abridged from his larger work (as above). Revised Edition. Square 12mo. 8s. 6d.

A **GREEK-ENGLISH LEXICON**. Compiled by H. G. LIDDELL, D.D. Dean of Christ Church, and R. SCOTT, D.D. Dean of Rochester. Sixth Edition. Crown 4to. price 36s.

A **Lexicon, Greek and English**, abridged from LIDDELL and SCOTT's *Greek-English Lexicon*. Twelfth Edition. Square 12mo. 7s. 6d.

A **SANSKRIT-ENGLISH DICTIONARY**, the Sanskrit words printed both in the original Devanagari and in Roman Letters. Compiled by T. BENFEY, Prof. in the Univ. of Göttingen. 8vo. 52s. 6d.

WALKER'S PRONOUNCING DICTIONARY of the ENGLISH LANGUAGE. Thoroughly revised Editions, by B. H. SMART. 8vo. 12s. 16mo. 6s.

A **PRACTICAL DICTIONARY of the FRENCH and ENGLISH LANGUAGES.** By L. CONTANSEAU. Fourteenth Edition. Post 8vo. 10s. 6d.

Contanseau's Pocket Dictionary, French and English, abridged from the above by the Author. New Edition, revised. Square 18mo. 3s. 6d.

NEW PRACTICAL DICTIONARY of the GERMAN LANGUAGE; German-English and English-German. By the Rev. W. L. BLACKLEY, M.A. and Dr. CARL MARTIN FRIEDLÄNDER. Post 8vo. 7s. 6d.

The **MASTERY of LANGUAGES**; or, the Art of Speaking Foreign Tongues Idiomatically. By THOMAS PRENDERGAST, late of the Civil Service at Madras. Second Edition. 8vo. 6s.

Miscellaneous Works and *Popular Metaphysics.*

The **ESSAYS and CONTRIBUTIONS of A. K. H. B.**, Author of ' The Recreations of a Country Parson.' Uniform Editions:—

Recreations of a Country Parson. By A. K. H. B. FIRST and SECOND SERIES, crown 8vo. 3s. 6d. each.

The **COMMON-PLACE PHILOSOPHER in TOWN and COUNTRY.** By A. K. H. B. Crown 8vo. price 3s. 6d.

Leisure Hours in Town; Essays Consolatory, Æsthetical, Moral, Social, and Domestic. By A. K. H. B. Crown 8vo. 3s. 6d.

The **Autumn Holidays of a Country Parson**; Essays contributed to *Fraser's Magazine* and to *Good Words*. By A. K. H. B. Crown 8vo. 3s. 6d.

The **Graver Thoughts of a Country Parson.** By A. K. H. B. FIRST and SECOND SERIES, crown 8vo. 3s. 6d. each.

Critical Essays of a Country Parson, selected from Essays contributed to *Fraser's Magazine*. By A. K. H. B. Crown 8vo. 3s. 6d.

Sunday Afternoons at the Parish Church of a Scottish University City. By A. K. H. B. Crown 8vo. 3s. 6d.

LESSONS of MIDDLE AGE; with some Account of various Cities and Men. By A. K. H. B. Crown 8vo. 3s. 6d.

Counsel and Comfort spoken from a City Pulpit. By A. K. H. B. Crown 8vo. price 3s. 6d.

Changed Aspects of Unchanged Truths; Memorials of St. Andrews Sundays. By A. K. H.B. Crown 8vo. 3s. 6d.

Present-day Thoughts; Memorials of St. Andrews Sundays. By A. K. H. B. Crown 8vo. 3s. 6d.

SHORT STUDIES on GREAT SUBJECTS. By JAMES ANTHONY FROUDE, M.A. late Fellow of Exeter Coll. Oxford. Third Edition. 8vo. 12s. SECOND SERIES. 8vo. price 12s.

LORD MACAULAY'S MISCELLANEOUS WRITINGS :—
LIBRARY EDITION. 2 vols. 8vo. Portrait, 21s.
PEOPLE'S EDITION. 1 vol. crown 8vo. 4s. 6d.

LORD MACAULAY'S MISCELLANEOUS WRITINGS and SPEECHES. STUDENT'S EDITION, in crown 8vo. price 6s.

The REV. SYDNEY SMITH'S MISCELLANEOUS WORKS; including his Contributions to the *Edinburgh Review.* Crown 8vo. 6s.

The Wit and Wisdom of the Rev. Sydney Smith; a Selection of the most memorable Passages in his Writings and Conversation. 16mo. 3s. 6d.

The ECLIPSE of FAITH; or, a Visit to a Religious Sceptic. By HENRY ROGERS. Twelfth Edition. Fcp. 5s.

Defence of the Eclipse of Faith, by its Author; a rejoinder to Dr. Newman's *Reply.* Third Edition. Fcp. 3s. 6d.

Selections from the Correspondence of R. E. H. Greyson. By the same Author. Third Edition. Crown 8vo. 7s. 6d.

FAMILIES of SPEECH, Four Lectures delivered at the Royal Institution of Great Britain. By the Rev. F. W. FARRAR, M.A. F.R.S. Head Master of Marlborough College. Post 8vo. with Two Maps, 5s. 6d.

CHIPS from a GERMAN WORKSHOP; being Essays on the Science of Religion, and on Mythology, Traditions, and Customs. By F. MAX MÜLLER, M.A. &c. Foreign Member of the French Institute. 3 vols. 8vo. £2.

UEBERWEG'S SYSTEM of LOGIC and HISTORY of LOGICAL DOCTRINES. Translated, with Notes and Appendices, by T. M. LINDSAY, M.A. F.R.S.E. Examiner in Philosophy to the University of Edinburgh. 8vo. price 16s.

ANALYSIS of the PHENOMENA of the HUMAN MIND. By JAMES MILL. A New Edition, with Notes, Illustrative and Critical, by ALEXANDER BAIN, ANDREW FINDLATER, and GEORGE GROTE. Edited, with additional Notes, by JOHN STUART MILL. 2 vols. 8vo. price 28s.

An INTRODUCTION to MENTAL PHILOSOPHY, on the Inductive Method. By J. D. MORELL, M.A. LL.D. 8vo. 12s.

ELEMENTS of PSYCHOLOGY, containing the Analysis of the Intellectual Powers. By the same Author. Post 8vo. 7s. 6d.

The SECRET of HEGEL: being the Hegelian System in Origin, Principle, Form, and Matter. By J. H. STIRLING. 2 vols. 8vo. 28s.

SIR WILLIAM HAMILTON; being the Philosophy of Perception: an Analysis. By J. H. STIRLING. 8vo. 5s.

The SENSES and the INTELLECT. By ALEXANDER BAIN, M.D. Professor of Logic in the University of Aberdeen. Third Edition. 8vo. 15s.

MENTAL and MORAL SCIENCE: a Compendium of Psychology and Ethics. By the same Author. Second Edition. Crown 8vo. 10s. 6d.

LOGIC, DEDUCTIVE and INDUCTIVE. By the same Author. In TWO PARTS, crown 8vo. 10s. 6d. Each Part may be had separately:— PART I. *Deduction*, 4s. PART II. *Induction*, 6s. 6d.

TIME and SPACE; a Metaphysical Essay. By SHADWORTH H. HODGSON. (This work covers the whole ground of Speculative Philosophy.) 8vo. price 16s.

The Theory of Practice; an Ethical Inquiry. By the same Author. (This work, in conjunction with the foregoing, completes a system of Philosophy.) 2 vols. 8vo. price 24s.

The PHILOSOPHY of NECESSITY; or, Natural Law as applicable to Mental, Moral, and Social Science. By CHARLES BRAY. Second Edition. 8vo. 9s.

The Education of the Feelings and Affections. By the same Author. Third Edition. 8vo. 3s. 6d.

On Force, its Mental and Moral Correlates. By the same Author. 8vo. 5s.

A TREATISE on HUMAN NATURE; being an Attempt to Introduce the Experimental Method of Reasoning into Moral Subjects. By DAVID HUME. Edited, with Notes, &c. by T. H. GREEN, Fellow, and T. H. GROSE, late Scholar, of Balliol College, Oxford.   [*In the press.*

ESSAYS MORAL, POLITICAL, and LITERARY. By DAVID HUME. By the same Editors.   [*In the press.*

Astronomy, Meteorology, Popular Geography, &c.

OUTLINES of ASTRONOMY. By Sir J. F. W. HERSCHEL, Bart. Eleventh Edition, with Plates and Woodcuts. Square crown 8vo. 12s.

The SUN; RULER, LIGHT, FIRE, and LIFE of the PLANETARY SYSTEM. By RICHARD A. PROCTOR, B.A. F.R.A.S. With 10 Plates (7 coloured) and 107 Figures on Wood. Crown 8vo. 14s.

OTHER WORLDS THAN OURS; the Plurality of Worlds Studied under the Light of Recent Scientific Researches. By the same Author. Second Edition, with 14 Illustrations. Crown 8vo. 10s. 6d.

SATURN and its SYSTEM. By the same Author. 8vo. with 14 Plates, 14s.

SCHALLEN'S SPECTRUM ANALYSIS, in its application to Terrestrial Substances and the Physical Constitution of the Heavenly Bodies. Translated by JANE and C. LASSELL; edited by W. HUGGINS, LL.D. F.R.S. Crown 8vo. with Illustrations.   [*Nearly ready.*

CELESTIAL OBJECTS for COMMON TELESCOPES. By the Rev.
T. W. WEBB, M.A. F.R.A.S. Second Edition, revised, with a large Map of
the Moon, and several Woodcuts. 16mo. 7s. 6d.

NAVIGATION and NAUTICAL ASTRONOMY (Practical, Theoretical,
Scientific) for the use of Students and Practical Men. By J. MERRIFIELD,
F.R.A.S and H. EVERS. 8vo. 14s.

DOVE'S LAW of STORMS, considered in connexion with the Ordinary
Movements of the Atmosphere. Translated by R. H. SCOTT, M.A. T.C.D.
8vo. 10s. 6d.

The CANADIAN DOMINION. By CHARLES MARSHALL. With 6
Illustrations on Wood. 8vo. price 12s. 6d.

A GENERAL DICTIONARY of GEOGRAPHY, Descriptive, Physical,
Statistical, and Historical : forming a complete Gazetteer of the World. By
A. KEITH JOHNSTON, LL.D. F.R.G.S. Revised Edition. 8vo. 31s. 6d.

A MANUAL of GEOGRAPHY, Physical, Industrial, and Political.
By W. HUGHES, F.R.G.S. With 6 Maps. Fcp. 7s. 6d.

MAUNDER'S TREASURY of GEOGRAPHY, Physical, Historical,
Descriptive, and Political. Edited by W. HUGHES, F.R.G.S. Revised
Edition, with 7 Maps and 16 Plates. Fcp. 6s. cloth, or 9s. 6d. bound in calf.

The PUBLIC SCHOOLS ATLAS of MODERN GEOGRAPHY. In
31 Maps, exhibiting clearly the more important Physical Features of the
Countries delineated, and Noting all the Chief Places of Historical, Commercial, or Social Interest. Edited, with an Introduction, by the Rev. G.
BUTLER, M.A. Imp. 4to. price 3s. 6d. sewed, or 5s. cloth. [Nearly ready.

Natural History and Popular Science.

ELEMENTARY TREATISE on PHYSICS, Experimental and Applied.
Translated and edited from GANOT's Eléments de Physique (with the
Author's sanction) by E. ATKINSON, Ph.D. F.C.S. New Edition, revised
and enlarged ; with a Coloured Plate and 620 Woodcuts. Post 8vo. 15s.

The ELEMENTS of PHYSICS or NATURAL PHILOSOPHY. By
NEIL ARNOTT, M.D. F.R.S. Physician Extraordinary to the Queen. Sixth
Edition, rewritten and completed. Two Parts. 8vo. 21s.

SOUND : a Course of Eight Lectures delivered at the Royal Institution
of Great Britain. By JOHN TYNDALL, LL.D. F.R.S. New Edition, crown
8vo. with Portrait of M. Chladni and 169 Woodcuts, price 9s.

HEAT a MODE of MOTION. By Professor JOHN TYNDALL, LL.D.
F.R.S. Fourth Edition. Crown 8vo. with Woodcuts, 10s. 6d.

RESEARCHES on DIAMAGNETISM and MAGNE-CRYSTALLIC
ACTION ; including the Question of Diamagnetic Polarity. By the same
Author. With 6 Plates and many Woodcuts. 8vo. price 14s.

PROFESSOR TYNDALL'S ESSAYS on the USE and LIMIT of the
IMAGINATION in SCIENCE. Being the Second Edition, with Additions,
of his Discourse on the Scientific Use of the Imagination. 8vo. 3s.

NOTES of a COURSE of SEVEN LECTURES on ELECTRICAL PHENOMENA and THEORIES, delivered at the Royal Institution, A.D. 1870. By Professor TYNDALL. Crown 8vo. 1s. sewed, or 1s. 6d. cloth.

NOTES of a COURSE of NINE LECTURES on LIGHT delivered at the Royal Institution, A.D. 1869. By the same Author. Crown 8vo. price 1s. sewed, or 1s. 6d. cloth.

FRAGMENTS of SCIENCE for UNSCIENTIFIC PEOPLE; a Series of detached Essays, Lectures, and Reviews. By JOHN TYNDALL, LL.D. F.R.S. Second Edition. 8vo. price 14s.

LIGHT SCIENCE for LEISURE HOURS; a Series of Familiar Essays on Scientific Subjects, Natural Phenomena, &c. By R. A. PROCTOR, B.A. F.R.A.S. Crown 8vo. price 7s. 6d.

LIGHT: Its Influence on Life and Health. By FORBES WINSLOW, M.D. D.C.L. Oxon. (Hon.). Fcp. 8vo. 6s.

A TREATISE on ELECTRICITY, in Theory and Practice. By A. DE LA RIVE, Prof. in the Academy of Geneva. Translated by C. V. WALKER, F.R.S. 3 vols. 8vo. with Woodcuts, £3 13s.

The BEGINNING: its When and its How. By MUNGO PONTON, F.R.S.E. Post 8vo. with very numerous Illustrations, price 18s.

The CORRELATION of PHYSICAL FORCES. By W. R. GROVE, Q.C. V.P.R.S. Fifth Edition, revised, and followed by a Discourse on Continuity. 8vo. 10s. 6d. The *Discourse on Continuity*, separately, 2s. 6d.

MANUAL of GEOLOGY. By S. HAUGHTON, M.D. F.R.S. Revised Edition, with 66 Woodcuts. Fcp. 7s. 6d.

VAN DER HOEVEN'S HANDBOOK of ZOOLOGY. Translated from the Second Dutch Edition by the Rev. W. CLARK, M.D. F.R.S. 2 vols. 8vo. with 24 Plates of Figures, 60s.

Professor OWEN'S LECTURES on the COMPARATIVE ANATOMY and Physiology of the Invertebrate Animals. Second Edition, with 235 Woodcuts. 8vo. 21s.

The COMPARATIVE ANATOMY and PHYSIOLOGY of the VERTE- brate Animals. By RICHARD OWEN, F.R.S. D.C.L. With 1,472 Woodcuts. 3 vols. 8vo. £3 13s. 6d.

The ORIGIN of CIVILISATION and the PRIMITIVE CONDITION of MAN; Mental and Social Condition of Savages. By Sir JOHN LUBBOCK, Bart. M.P. F.R.S. Second Edition, with 25 Woodcuts. 8vo. price 16s.

The PRIMITIVE INHABITANTS of SCANDINAVIA: containing a Description of the Implements, Dwellings, Tombs, and Mode of Living of the Savages in the North of Europe during the Stone Age. By SVEN NILSSON. With 16 Plates of Figures and 3 Woodcuts. 8vo. 18s.

BIBLE ANIMALS; being a Description of every Living Creature mentioned in the Scriptures, from the Ape to the Coral. By the Rev. J. G. WOOD, M.A. F.L.S. With about 100 Vignettes on Wood. 8vo. 21s.

HOMES WITHOUT HANDS: a Description of the Habitations of Animals, classed according to their Principle of Construction. By Rev. J. G. WOOD, M.A. F.L.S. With about 140 Vignettes on Wood, 8vo. 21s.

INSECTS AT HOME. By the Rev. J. G. Wood, M.A. F.L.S. With a Frontispiece in Colours, 21 full-page Illustrations, and about 700 smaller Illustrations from original designs engraved on Wood by G. Pearson. 8vo. price 21s.

STRANGE DWELLINGS; being a description of the Habitations of Animals, abridged from 'Homes without Hands.' By J. G. Wood, M.A. F.L.S. With a New Frontispiece and about 60 other Woodcut Illustrations. Crown 8vo. price 7s. 6d.

A FAMILIAR HISTORY of BIRDS. By E. Stanley, D.D. F.R.S. late Lord Bishop of Norwich. Seventh Edition, with Woodcuts. Fcp. 3s. 6d.

The HARMONIES of NATURE and UNITY of CREATION. By Dr. George Hartwig. 8vo. with numerous Illustrations, 18s.

The SEA and its LIVING WONDERS. By the same Author. Third (English) Edition. 8vo. with many Illustrations, 21s.

The TROPICAL WORLD. By Dr. Geo. Hartwig. With 8 Chromoxylographs and 172 Woodcuts. 8vo. 21s.

The SUBTERRANEAN WORLD. By Dr. George Hartwig. With 3 Maps and about 80 Woodcuts, including 8 full size of page. 8vo. price 21s.

The POLAR WORLD, a Popular Description of Man and Nature in the Arctic and Antarctic Regions of the Globe. By Dr. George Hartwig. With 8 Chromoxylographs, 3 Maps, and 85 Woodcuts. 8vo. 21s.

KIRBY and SPENCE'S INTRODUCTION to ENTOMOLOGY, or Elements of the Natural History of Insects. 7th Edition. Crown 8vo. 5s.

MAUNDER'S TREASURY of NATURAL HISTORY, or Popular Dictionary of Zoology. Revised and corrected by T. S. Cobbold, M.D. Fcp. with 900 Woodcuts, 6s. cloth, or 9s. 6d. bound in calf.

The TREASURY of BOTANY, or Popular Dictionary of the Vegetable Kingdom; including a Glossary of Botanical Terms. Edited by J. Lindley, F.R.S. and T. Moore, F.L.S. assisted by eminent Contributors. With 274 Woodcuts and 20 Steel Plates. Two Parts, fcp. 12s. cloth, or 19s. calf.

The ELEMENTS of BOTANY for FAMILIES and SCHOOLS. Tenth Edition, revised by Thomas Moore, F.L.S. Fcp. with 154 Woodcuts, 2s. 6d.

The ROSE AMATEUR'S GUIDE. By Thomas Rivers. Ninth Edition. Fcp. 4s.

LOUDON'S ENCYCLOPÆDIA of PLANTS; comprising the Specific Character, Description, Culture, History, &c. of all the Plants found in Great Britain. With upwards of 12,000 Woodcuts. 8vo. 42s.

MAUNDER'S SCIENTIFIC and LITERARY TREASURY. New Edition, thoroughly revised and in great part re-written, with above 1,000 new Articles, by J. Y. Johnson, Corr. M.Z.S. Fcp. 6s. cloth, or 9s. 6d. calf.

A DICTIONARY of SCIENCE, LITERATURE, and ART. Fourth Edition, re-edited by W. T. Brande (the original Author), and George W. Cox, M.A. assisted by contributors of eminent Scientific and Literary Acquirements. 3 vols. medium 8vo. price 63s. cloth.

Chemistry, Medicine, Surgery, and the Allied Sciences.

A DICTIONARY of CHEMISTRY and the Allied Branches of other Sciences. By HENRY WATTS, F.R.S. assisted by eminent Contributors Complete in 5 vols. medium 8vo. £7 3s.

ELEMENTS of CHEMISTRY, Theoretical and Practical. By W. ALLEN MILLER, M.D. late Prof. of Chemistry, King's Coll. London. Fourth Edition. 3 vols. 8vo. £3. PART I. CHEMICAL PHYSICS, 15s. PART II. INORGANIC CHEMISTRY, 21s. PART III. ORGANIC CHEMISTRY, 24s.

A MANUAL of CHEMISTRY, Descriptive and Theoretical. By WILLIAM ODLING, M.B. F.R.S. PART I. 8vo. 9s. PART II. *just ready.*

OUTLINES of CHEMISTRY; or, Brief Notes of Chemical Facts. By WILLIAM ODLING, M.B. F.R.S. Crown 8vo. 7s. 6d.

A Course of Practical Chemistry, for the use of Medical Students. By the same Author. New Edition, with 70 Woodcuts. Crown 8vo. 7s. 6d.

Lectures on Animal Chemistry, delivered at the Royal College of Physicians in 1865. By the same Author. Crown 8vo. 4s. 6d.

Lectures on the Chemical Changes of Carbon. Delivered at the Royal Institution of Great Britain. By the same Author. Crown 8vo. price 4s. 6d.

SELECT METHODS in CHEMICAL ANALYSIS, chiefly INORGANIC. By WILLIAM CROOKES, F.R.S. With 22 Woodcuts. Crown 8vo. price 12s. 6d.

A TREATISE on MEDICAL ELECTRICITY, THEORETICAL and PRACTICAL; and its Use in the Treatment of Paralysis, Neuralgia, and other Diseases. By JULIUS ALTHAUS, M.D. &c. Second Edition, revised and partly re-written. Post 8vo. with Plate and 2 Woodcuts, price 15s.

The DIAGNOSIS, PATHOLOGY, and TREATMENT of DISEASES of Women; including the Diagnosis of Pregnancy. By GRAILY HEWITT, M.D. Second Edition, enlarged; with 116 Woodcut Illustrations. 8vo. 24s.

On SOME DISORDERS of the NERVOUS SYSTEM in CHILD-HOOD; being the Lumleian Lectures delivered before the Royal College of Physicians in March 1871. By CHARLES WEST, M.D. Crown 8vo. price 5s.

LECTURES on the DISEASES of INFANCY and CHILDHOOD. By CHARLES WEST, M.D. &c. Fifth Edition, revised and enlarged. 8vo. 16s.

A SYSTEM of SURGERY, Theoretical and Practical. In Treatises by Various Authors. Edited by T. HOLMES, M.A. &c. Surgeon and Lecturer on Surgery at St. George's Hospital, and Surgeon-in-Chief to the Metropolitan Police. Second Edition, thoroughly revised, with numerous Illustrations. 5 vols. 8vo. £5 5s.

The SURGICAL TREATMENT of CHILDREN'S DISEASES. By T. HOLMES, M.A. &c. late Surgeon to the Hospital for Sick Children. Second Edition, with 9 Plates and 112 Woodcuts. 8vo. 21s.

LECTURES on the PRINCIPLES and PRACTICE of PHYSIC. By Sir THOMAS WATSON, Bart. M.D. Fifth Edition, thoroughly revised. 2 vols. 8vo. price 36s.

LECTURES on SURGICAL PATHOLOGY. By Sir JAMES PAGET, Bart. F.R.S. Third Edition, revised and re-edited by the Author and Professor W. TURNER, M.B. 8vo. with 131 Woodcuts, 21s.

COOPER'S DICTIONARY of PRACTICAL SURGERY and Encyclopædia of Surgical Science. New Edition, brought down to the present time. By S. A. LANE, Surgeon to St. Mary's Hospital, assisted by various Eminent Surgeons. VOL. II. 8vo. completing the work. [*In the press.*

On **CHRONIC BRONCHITIS,** especially as connected with **GOUT,** EMPHYSEMA, and DISEASES of the HEART. By E. HEADLAM GREENHOW, M.D. F.R.C.P. &c. 8vo. 7s. 6d.

The **CLIMATE of the SOUTH of FRANCE as SUITED to INVALIDS;** with Notices of Mediterranean and other Winter Stations. By C. T. WILLIAMS, M.A. M.D. Oxon. Assistant-Physician to the Hospital for Consumption at Brompton. Second Edition. Crown 8vo. 6s.

REPORTS on the PROGRESS of PRACTICAL and SCIENTIFIC MEDICINE in Different Parts of the World. Edited by HORACE DOBELL, M.D. assisted by numerous and distinguished Coadjutors. Vols. I. and II. 8vo. 18s. each.

PULMONARY CONSUMPTION; its Nature, Varieties, and Treatment: with an Analysis of One Thousand Cases to exemplify its Duration. By C. J. B. WILLIAMS, M.D. F.R.S. and C. T. WILLIAMS, M.A. M.D. Oxon. Post 8vo. price 10s. 6d.

CLINICAL LECTURES on DISEASES of the LIVER, JAUNDICE, and ABDOMINAL DROPSY. By CHARLES MURCHISON, M.D. Post 8vo. with 25 Woodcuts, 10s. 6d.

ANATOMY, DESCRIPTIVE and SURGICAL. By HENRY GRAY, F.R.S. With about 400 Woodcuts from Dissections. Fifth Edition, by T. HOLMES, M.A. Cantab. with a new Introduction by the Editor. Royal 8vo. 28s.

CLINICAL NOTES on DISEASES of the LARYNX, investigated and treated with the assistance of the Laryngoscope. By W. MARCET, M.D. F.R.S. Crown 8vo. with 5 Lithographs, 6s.

OUTLINES of PHYSIOLOGY, Human and Comparative. By JOHN MARSHALL, F.R.C.S. Surgeon to the University College Hospital. 2 vols. crown 8vo. with 122 Woodcuts, 32s.

PHYSIOLOGICAL ANATOMY and PHYSIOLOGY of MAN. By the late R. B. TODD, M.D. F.R.S. and W. BOWMAN, F.R.S. of King's College. With numerous Illustrations. VOL. II. 8vo. 25s.
VOL. I. New Edition by Dr. LIONEL S. BEALE. F.R.S. in course of publication, with many Illustrations. PARTS I. and II. price 7s. 6d. each.

COPLAND'S DICTIONARY of PRACTICAL MEDICINE, abridged from the larger work and throughout brought down to the present State of Medical Science. 8vo. 36s.

REIMANN'S HANDBOOK of ANILINE and its **DERIVATIVES;** a Treatise on the Manufacture of Aniline and Aniline Colours. Edited by WILLIAM CROOKES, F.R.S. With 5 Woodcuts. 8vo. 10s. 6d.

On the **MANUFACTURE of BEET-ROOT SUGAR in ENGLAND** and IRELAND. By WILLIAM CROOKES, F.R.S. Crown 8vo. with 11 Woodcuts, 8s. 6d.

A MANUAL of MATERIA MEDICA and THERAPEUTICS, abridged from Dr. PEREIRA'S *Elements* by F. J. FARRE, M.D. assisted by R. BENTLEY, M.R.C.S. and by R. WARINGTON, F.R.S. 8vo. with 90 Woodcuts, 21s.

THOMSON'S CONSPECTUS of the BRITISH PHARMACOPŒIA. 25th Edition, corrected by E. LLOYD BIRKETT, M.D. 18mo. price 6s.

The Fine Arts, and *Illustrated Editions.*

IN FAIRYLAND; Pictures from the Elf-World. By RICHARD DOYLE. With a Poem by W. ALLINGHAM. With Sixteen Plates, containing Thirty-six Designs printed in Colours. Folio, 31s. 6d.

LIFE of JOHN GIBSON, R.A. SCULPTOR. Edited by Lady EASTLAKE. 8vo. 10s. 6d.

MATERIALS for a HISTORY of OIL PAINTING. By Sir CHARLES LOCKE EASTLAKE, sometime President of the Royal Academy. 2 vols. 8vo. price 30s.

HALF-HOUR LECTURES on the HISTORY and PRACTICE of the Fine and Ornamental Arts. By WILLIAM B. SCOTT. New Edition, revised by the Author; with 50 Woodcuts. Crown 8vo. 8s. 6d.

ALBERT DURER, HIS LIFE and WORKS; including Autobiographical Papers and Complete Catalogues. By WILLIAM B. SCOTT. With Six Etchings by the Author, and other Illustrations. 8vo. 16s.

SIX LECTURES on HARMONY, delivered at the Royal Institution of Great Britain in the Year 1867. By G. A. MACFARREN. With numerous engraved Musical Examples and Specimens. 8vo. 10s. 6d.

The CHORALE BOOK for ENGLAND: the Hymns translated by Miss C. WINKWORTH; the Tunes arranged by Prof. W. S. BENNETT and OTTO GOLDSCHMIDT. Fcp. 4to. 12s. 6d.

The NEW TESTAMENT, illustrated with Wood Engravings after the Early Masters, chiefly of the Italian School. Crown 4to. 63s. cloth, gilt top; or £5 5s. elegantly bound in morocco.

LYRA GERMANICA; the Christian Year. Translated by CATHERINE WINKWORTH; with 125 Illustrations on Wood drawn by J. LEIGHTON, F.S.A. 4to. 21s.

LYRA GERMANICA; the Christian Life. Translated by CATHERINE WINKWORTH; with about 200 Woodcut Illustrations by J. LEIGHTON, F.S.A. and other Artists. 4to. 21s.

The LIFE of MAN SYMBOLISED by the MONTHS of the YEAR. Text selected by R. PIGOT; Illustrations on Wood from Original Designs by J. LEIGHTON, F.S.A. 4to. 42s.

CATS' and FARLIE'S MORAL EMBLEMS; with Aphorisms, Adages, and Proverbs of all Nations. 121 Illustrations on Wood by J. LEIGHTON, F.S.A. Text selected by R. PIGOT. Imperial 8vo. 31s. 6d.

SACRED and **LEGENDARY ART.** By Mrs. JAMESON.

Legends of the Saints and Martyrs. Fifth Edition, with 19
Etchings and 187 Woodcuts. 2 vols. square crown 8vo. 31s. 6d.

Legends of the Monastic Orders. Third Edition, with 11 Etchings
and 88 Woodcuts. 1 vol. square crown 8vo. 21s.

Legends of the Madonna. Third Edition, with 27 Etchings and 165
Woodcuts. 1 vol. square crown 8vo. 21s.

The History of Our Lord, with that of his Types and Precursors.
Completed by Lady EASTLAKE. Revised Edition, with 31 Etchings and
281 Woodcuts. 2 vols. square crown 8vo. 42s.

— —

The Useful Arts, Manufactures, &c.

HISTORY of the GOTHIC REVIVAL; an Attempt to shew how far
the taste for Mediæval Architecture was retained in England during the
last two centuries, and has been re-developed in the present. By CHARLES L.
EASTLAKE, Architect. With many Illustrations. Imp. 8vo. price 31s. 6d.

GWILT'S ENCYCLOPÆDIA of ARCHITECTURE, with above 1,600
Engravings on Wood. Fifth Edition, revised and enlarged by WYATT
PAPWORTH. 8vo. 52s. 6d.

A MANUAL of ARCHITECTURE: being a Concise History and
Explanation of the principal Styles of European Architecture, Ancient,
Mediæval, and Renaissance; with a Glossary of Technical Terms. By
THOMAS MITCHELL. Crown 8vo. with 150 Woodcuts, 10s. 6d.

ITALIAN SCULPTORS; being a History of Sculpture in Northern,
Southern, and Eastern Italy. By C. C. PERKINS. With 30 Etchings and
13 Wood Engravings. Imperial 8vo. 42s.

TUSCAN SCULPTORS, their Lives, Works, and Times. With 45
Etchings and 28 Woodcuts from Original Drawings and Photographs. By
the same Author. 2 vols. imperial 8vo. 63s.

HINTS on HOUSEHOLD TASTE in FURNITURE, UPHOLSTERY,
and other Details. By CHARLES L. EASTLAKE, Architect. Second Edition,
with about 90 Illustrations. Square crown 8vo. 18s.

The ENGINEER'S HANDBOOK; explaining the Principles which
should guide the Young Engineer in the Construction of Machinery. By
C. S. LOWNDES. Post 8vo. 5s.

PRINCIPLES of MECHANISM, designed for the Use of Students in
the Universities, and for Engineering Students generally. By R.
WILLIS, M.A. F.R.S. &c. Jacksonian Professor in the University of Cambridge. Second Edition, enlarged; with 374 Woodcuts. 8vo. 18s.

LATHES and TURNING, Simple, Mechanical, and ORNAMENTAL.
By W. HENRY NORTHCOTT. With about 240 Illustrations on Steel and
Wood. 8vo. 18s.

URE'S DICTIONARY of ARTS, MANUFACTURES, and MINES.
Sixth Edition, chiefly rewritten and greatly enlarged by ROBERT HUNT,
F.R.S. assisted by numerous Contributors eminent in Science and the
Arts, and familiar with Manufactures. With above 2,000 Woodcuts. 3 vols.
medium 8vo. price £4 14s. 6d.

B

HANDBOOK of PRACTICAL TELEGRAPHY. By R. S. CULLEY, Memb. Inst. C.E. Engineer-in-Chief of Telegraphs to the Post Office. Fifth Edition, with 118 Woodcuts and 9 Plates. 8vo. price 14s.

ENCYCLOPÆDIA of CIVIL ENGINEERING, Historical, Theoretical, and Practical. By E. CRESY, C.E. With above 3,000 Woodcuts. 8vo. 42s.

TREATISE on MILLS and MILLWORK. By Sir W. FAIRBAIRN, Bart. F.R.S. New Edition, with 18 Plates and 322 Woodcuts. 2 vols. 8vo. 32s.

USEFUL INFORMATION for ENGINEERS. By the same Author. FIRST, SECOND, and THIRD SERIES, with many Plates and Woodcuts, 3 vols. crown 8vo. 10s. 6d. each.

The **APPLICATION of CAST and WROUGHT IRON to** Building Purposes. By Sir W. FAIRBAIRN, Bart. F.R.S. Fourth Edition, enlarged; with 6 Plates and 118 Woodcuts. 8vo. price 16s.

IRON SHIP BUILDING, its History and Progress, as comprised in a Series of Experimental Researches. By the same Author. With 4 Plates and 130 Woodcuts. 8vo. 18s.

A TREATISE on the STEAM ENGINE, in its various Applications to Mines, Mills, Steam Navigation, Railways and Agriculture. By J. BOURNE, C.E. Eighth Edition; with Portrait, 37 Plates, and 546 Woodcuts. 4to. 42s.

CATECHISM of the STEAM ENGINE, in its various Applications to Mines, Mills, Steam Navigation, Railways, and Agriculture. By the same Author. With 89 Woodcuts. Fcp. 6s.

HANDBOOK of the STEAM ENGINE. By the same Author, forming a KEY to the Catechism of the Steam Engine, with 67 Woodcuts. Fcp. 9s.

BOURNE'S RECENT IMPROVEMENTS in the STEAM ENGINE in its various applications to Mines, Mills, Steam Navigation, Railways, and Agriculture. Being a Supplement to the Author's 'Catechism of the Steam Engine.' By JOHN BOURNE, C.E. New Edition, including many New Examples; with 124 Woodcuts. Fcp. 8vo. 6s.

A TREATISE on the SCREW PROPELLER, SCREW VESSELS, and Screw Engines, as adapted for purposes of Peace and War; with Notices of other Methods of Propulsion, Tables of the Dimensions and Performance of Screw Steamers, and detailed Specifications of Ships and Engines. By J. BOURNE, C.E. New Edition, with 54 Plates and 287 Woodcuts. 4to. 63s.

EXAMPLES of MODERN STEAM, AIR, and GAS ENGINES of the most Approved Types, as employed for Pumping, for Driving Machinery, for Locomotion, and for Agriculture, minutely and practically described. By JOHN BOURNE, C.E. In course of publication in 24 Parts, price 2s. 6d. each, forming One volume 4to. with about 50 Plates and 400 Woodcuts.'

A HISTORY of the MACHINE-WROUGHT HOSIERY and LACE Manufactures. By WILLIAM FELKIN, F.L.S. F.S.S. Royal 8vo. 21s.

PRACTICAL TREATISE on METALLURGY, adapted from the last German Edition of Professor KERL's *Metallurgy* by W. CROOKES, F.R.S. &c. and E. RÖHRIG, Ph.D. M.E. With 625 Woodcuts. 3 vols. 8vo. price £4 19s.

MITCHELL'S MANUAL of PRACTICAL ASSAYING. Third Edition, for the most part re-written, with all the recent Discoveries incorporated, by W. CROOKES, F.R.S. With 188 Woodcuts. 8vo. 28s.

The **ART of PERFUMERY**; the History and Theory of Odours, and the Methods of Extracting the Aromas of Plants. By Dr. PIESSE, F.C.S. Third Edition, with 53 Woodcuts. Crown 8vo. 10s. 6d.

Chemical, Natural, and Physical Magic, for Juveniles during the Holidays. By the same Author. Third Edition, with 38 Woodcuts. Fcp. 6s.

LOUDON'S ENCYCLOPÆDIA of AGRICULTURE: comprising the Laying-out, Improvement, and Management of Landed Property, and the Cultivation and Economy of the Productions of Agriculture. With 1,100 Woodcuts. 8vo. 21s.

Loudon's Encyclopædia of Gardening: comprising the Theory and Practice of Horticulture, Floriculture, Arboriculture, and Landscape Gardening. With 1,000 Woodcuts. 8vo. 21s.

BAYLDON'S ART of VALUING RENTS and TILLAGES, and Claims of Tenants upon Quitting Farms, both at Michaelmas and Lady-Day. Eighth Edition, revised by J. C. MORTON. 8vo. 10s. 6d.

Religious and *Moral Works.*

OLD TESTAMENT SYNONYMS, their BEARING on CHRISTIAN FAITH and PRACTICE. By the Rev. R. B. GIRDLESTONE, M.A. 8vo.
[*Nearly ready.*

An **INTRODUCTION to the THEOLOGY of the CHURCH of ENGLAND**, in an Exposition of the Thirty-nine Articles. By the Rev. T. P. BOULTBEE, M.A. Fcp. 8vo. price 6s.

FUNDAMENTALS; or, Bases of Belief concerning MAN and GOD: a Handbook of Mental, Moral, and Religious Philosophy. By the Rev. T. GRIFFITH, M.A. 8vo. price 10s. 6d.

PRAYERS SELECTED from the COLLECTION of the late BARON BUNSEN, and Translated by CATHERINE WINKWORTH. PART I. For the Family. PART II. Prayers and Meditations for Private Use. Fcp. 8vo. price 3s. 6d.

The **STUDENT'S COMPENDIUM of the BOOK of COMMON PRAYER**; being Notes Historical and Explanatory of the Liturgy of the Church of England. By the Rev. H. ALLDEN NASH. Fcp. 8vo. price 2s. 6d.

The **BIBLE and POPULAR THEOLOGY**; a Re-statement of Truths and Principles, with special reference to recent works of Dr. Liddon, Lord Hatherley, and the Right Hon. W. E. Gladstone. By G. VANCE SMITH, B.A. Ph.D. 8vo. price 7s. 6d.

The **TRUTH of the BIBLE**: Evidence from the Mosaic and other Records of Creation; the Origin and Antiquity of Man; the Science of Scripture; and from the Archæology of Different Nations of the Earth. By the Rev. B. W. SAVILE, M.A. Crown 8vo. price 7s. 6d.

CHURCHES and their CREEDS. By the Rev. Sir PHILIP PERRING, Bart. late Scholar of Trin. Coll. Cambridge, and University Medallist. Crown 8vo. price 10s. 6d.

CONSIDERATIONS on the REVISION of the ENGLISH NEW TESTAMENT. By C. J. ELLICOTT, D.D. Lord Bishop of Gloucester and Bristol. Post 8vo. price 5s. 6d.

An **EXPOSITION of the 39 ARTICLES**, Historical and Doctrinal. By E. HAROLD BROWNE, D.D. Lord Bishop of Ely. Ninth Edit. 8vo. 16s.

The LIFE and EPISTLES of ST. PAUL. By the Rev. W. J.
CONYBEARE, M.A., and the Very Rev. J. S. HOWSON, D.D. Dean of Chester:—
LIBRARY EDITION, with all the Original Illustrations, Maps, Landscapes
on Steel, Woodcuts, &c. 2 vols. 4to. 48s.

INTERMEDIATE EDITION, with a Selection of Maps, Plates, and Woodcuts.
2 vols. square crown 8vo. 31s. 6d.

STUDENT'S EDITION, revised and condensed, with 46 Illustrations and
Maps. 1 vol. crown 8vo. price 9s.

The VOYAGE and SHIPWRECK of ST. PAUL; with Dissertations
on the Life and Writings of St. Luke and the Ships and Navigation of the
Ancients. By JAMES SMITH, F.R.S. Third Edition. Crown 8vo. 10s. 6d.

A CRITICAL and GRAMMATICAL COMMENTARY on ST. PAUL'S
Epistles. By C. J. ELLICOTT, D.D. Lord Bishop of Gloucester & Bristol. 8vo.

Galatians, Fourth Edition, 8s. 6d.

Ephesians, Fourth Edition, 8s. 6d.

Pastoral Epistles, Fourth Edition, 10s. 6d.

Philippians, Colossians, and Philemon, Third Edition, 10s. 6d.

Thessalonians, Third Edition, 7s. 6d.

HISTORICAL LECTURES on the LIFE of OUR LORD JESUS
CHRIST: being the Hulsean Lectures for 1859. By C. J. ELLICOTT, D.D.
Lord Bishop of Gloucester and Bristol. Fifth Edition. 8vo. price 12s.

EVIDENCE of the TRUTH of the CHRISTIAN RELIGION derived
from the Literal Fulfilment of Prophecy. By ALEXANDER KEITH, D.D.
37th Edition, with numerous Plates, in square 8vo. 12s. 6d.; also the 39th
Edition, in post 8vo. with 5 Plates, 6s.

History and Destiny of the World and Church, according to
Scripture. By the same Author. Square 8vo. with 40 Illustrations, 10s.

An INTRODUCTION to the STUDY of the NEW TESTAMENT,
Critical, Exegetical, and Theological. By the Rev. S. DAVIDSON, D.D.
LL.D. 2 vols. 8vo. 30s.

HARTWELL HOENE'S INTRODUCTION to the CRITICAL STUDY
and Knowledge of the Holy Scriptures, as last revised; with 4 Maps and
22 Woodcuts and Facsimiles. 4 vols. 8vo. 42s.

Horne's Compendious Introduction to the Study of the Bible. Re-
edited by the Rev. JOHN AYRE, M.A. With Maps, &c. Post 8vo. 6s.

EWALD'S HISTORY of ISRAEL to the DEATH of MOSES. Translated from the German. Edited, with a Preface and an Appendix, by RUSSELL
MARTINEAU, M.A. Second Edition. 2 vols. 8vo. 24s.

The HISTORY and LITERATURE of the ISRAELITES, according
to the Old Testament and the Apocrypha. By C. DE ROTHSCHILD and
A. DE ROTHSCHILD. Second Edition, revised. 2 vols. post 8vo. with Two
Maps, price 12s. 6d.

The SEE of ROME in the MIDDLE AGES. By the Rev. OSWALD
J. REICHEL, B.C.L. and M.A. 8vo. price 18s.

The TREASURY of BIBLE KNOWLEDGE; being a Dictionary of the
Books, Persons, Places, Events, and other matters of which mention is made
in Holy Scripture. By Rev. J. AYRE, M.A. With Maps. 16 Plates, and
numerous Woodcuts. Fcp. 8vo price 6s. cloth, or 9s. 6d. neatly bound in calf.

The **GREEK TESTAMENT**; with Notes, Grammatical and Exegetical. By the Rev. W. WEBSTER, M.A. and the Rev. W. F. WILKINSON, M.A. 2 vols. 8vo. £2 4s.

EVERY-DAY SCRIPTURE DIFFICULTIES explained and illustrated. By J. E. PRESCOTT, M.A. VOL. I. *Matthew* and *Mark*; VOL. II. *Luke* and *John*. 2 vols. 8vo. 9s. each.

The **PENTATEUCH and BOOK of JOSHUA CRITICALLY EXAMINED.** By the Right Rev. J. W. COLENSO, D.D. Lord Bishop of Natal. People's Edition, in 1 vol. crown 8vo. 6s.

SIX SERMONS on the **FOUR CARDINAL VIRTUES** in relation to the Public and Private Life of Catholics. By the Rev. ORBY SHIPLEY, M.A. Crown 8vo. with Frontispiece, price 7s. 6d.

The **FORMATION** of **CHRISTENDOM.** By T. W. ALLIES. PARTS I. and II. 8vo. price 12s. each Part.

ENGLAND and **CHRISTENDOM.** By ARCHBISHOP MANNING, D.D. Post 8vo. price 10s. 6d.

CHRISTENDOM'S DIVISIONS, PART I., a Philosophical Sketch of the Divisions of the Christian Family in East and West. By EDMUND S. FFOULKES. Post 8vo. price 7s. 6d.

Christendom's Divisions, PART II. Greeks and Latins, being a History of their Dissensions and Overtures for Peace down to the Reformation. By the same Author. Post 8vo. 15s.

A VIEW of the SCRIPTURE REVELATIONS CONCERNING a FUTURE STATE. By RICHARD WHATELY, D.D. late Archbishop of Dublin. Ninth Edition. Fcp. 8vo. 5s.

THOUGHTS for the AGE. By ELIZABETH M. SEWELL, Author of 'Amy Herbert' &c. New Edition, revised. Fcp. 8vo. price 5s.

Passing Thoughts on Religion. By the same Author. Fcp. 8vo. 5s.

Self-Examination before Confirmation. By the same Author. 32mo. price 1s. 6d.

Readings for a Month Preparatory to Confirmation, from Writers of the Early and English Church. By the same Author. Fcp. 4s.

Readings for Every Day in Lent, compiled from the Writings of Bishop JEREMY TAYLOR. By the same Author. Fcp. 5s.

Preparation for the Holy Communion; the Devotions chiefly from the works of JEREMY TAYLOR. By the same Author. 32mo. 3s.

THOUGHTS for the HOLY WEEK for Young Persons. By the Author of 'Amy Herbert.' New Edition. Fcp. 8vo. 2s.

PRINCIPLES of EDUCATION Drawn from Nature and Revelation, and applied to Female Education in the Upper Classes. By the Author of 'Amy Herbert.' 2 vols. fcp. 12s. 6d.

SINGERS and SONGS of the CHURCH: being Biographical Sketches of the Hymn-Writers in all the principal Collections; with Notes on their Psalms and Hymns. By JOSIAH MILLER, M.A. Post 8vo. price 10s. 6d.

LYRA GERMANICA, translated from the German by Miss C. WINKWORTH. FIRST SERIES, Hymns for the Sundays and Chief Festivals. SECOND SERIES, the Christian Life. Fcp. 3s. 6d. each SERIES.

'SPIRITUAL SONGS' for the SUNDAYS and HOLIDAYS throughout the Year. By J. S. B. MONSELL, LL.D. Vicar of Egham and Rural Dean.
Fourth Edition, Sixth Thousand. Fcp. 4s. 6d.

The BEATITUDES: Abasement before God ; Sorrow for Sin ; Meekness
of Spirit ; Desire for Holiness ; Gentleness ; Purity of Heart ; the Peace-
makers ; Sufferings for Christ. By the same. Third Edition. Fcp. 3s. 6d.

His PRESENCE—not his MEMORY, 1855. By the same Author,
in Memory of his Son. Sixth Edition. 16mo. 1s.

LYRA EUCHARISTICA ; Hymns and Verses on the Holy Communion,
Ancient and Modern: with other Poems. Edited by the Rev. ORBY SHIP-
LEY, M.A. Second Edition. Fcp. 5s.

Lyra Messianica ; Hymns and Verses on the Life of Christ, Ancient
and Modern ; with other Poems. By the same Editor. Second Edition,
altered and enlarged. Fcp. 5s.

Lyra Mystica ; Hymns and Verses on Sacred Subjects, Ancient and
Modern. By the same Editor. Fcp. 5s.

ENDEAVOURS after the CHRISTIAN LIFE : Discourses. By
JAMES MARTINEAU. Fourth Edition, carefully revised. Post 8vo. 7s. 6d.

INVOCATION of SAINTS and ANGELS, for the use of Members of
the English Church. Edited by the Rev. ORBY SHIPLEY. 24mo. 3s. 6d.

WHATELY'S INTRODUCTORY LESSONS on the CHRISTIAN
Evidences. 18mo. 6d.

FOUR DISCOURSES of CHRYSOSTOM, chiefly on the Parable of the
Rich Man and Lazarus. Translated by F. ALLEN, B.A. Crown 8vo. 3s. 6d.

BISHOP JEREMY TAYLOR'S ENTIRE WORKS. With Life by
BISHOP HEBER. Revised and corrected by the Rev. C. P. EDEN, 10 vols.
price £5 5s.

Travels, Voyages, &c.

HOW to SEE NORWAY. By Captain J. R. CAMPBELL. With Map
and 5 Woodcuts. Fcp. 8vo. price 5s.

PAU and the PYRENEES. By Count HENRY RUSSELL, Member of
the Alpine Club, &c. With 2 Maps. Fcp. 8vo. price 5s.

SCENES in the SUNNY SOUTH; including the Atlas Mountains
and the Oases of the Sahara in Algeria. By Lieut.-Col. the Hon. C. S.
VEREKER, M.A. Commandant of the Limerick Artillery Militia. 2 vols.
post 8vo. price 21s.

The PLAYGROUND of EUROPE. By LESLIE STEPHEN, late President
of the Alpine Club. With 4 Illustrations engraved on Wood by E. Whymper.
Crown 8vo. price 10s. 6d.

CADORE ; or, TITIAN'S COUNTRY. By JOSIAH GILBERT, one of
the Authors of 'The Dolomite Mountains.' With Map, Facsimile, and 40
Illustrations. Imperial 8vo. 31s. 6d.

HOURS of EXERCISE in the ALPS. By JOHN TYNDALL, LL.D.
F.R.S. Second Edition, with 7 Woodcuts by E. Whymper. Crown 8vo.
price 12s. 6d.

TRAVELS in the CENTRAL CAUCASUS and BASHAN. Including Visits to Ararat and Tabreez and Ascents of Kazbek and Elbruz. By D. W. FRESHFIELD. Square crown 8vo. with Maps, &c. 18s.

PICTURES in TYROL and Elsewhere. From a Family Sketch-Book. By the Authoress of 'A Voyage en Zigzag,' &c. Second Edition. Small 4to. with numerous Illustrations, 21s.

HOW WE SPENT the SUMMER; or, a Voyage en Zigzag in Switzerland and Tyrol with some Members of the ALPINE CLUB. From the Sketch-Book of one of the Party. In oblong 4to. with 300 Illustrations, 15s.

BEATEN TRACKS; or, Pen and Pencil Sketches in Italy. By the Authoress of 'A Voyage en Zigzag.' With 42 Plates, containing about 200 Sketches from Drawings made on the Spot. 8vo. 16s.

MAP of the CHAIN of MONT BLANC, from an actual Survey in 1863—1864. By A. ADAMS-REILLY, F.R.G.S. M.A.C. Published under the Authority of the Alpine Club. In Chromolithography on extra stout drawing-paper 28in. × 17in. price 10s. or mounted on canvas in a folding case, 12s. 6d.

WESTWARD by RAIL; the New Route to the East. By W. F. RAE. With Map shewing the Lines of Rail between the Atlantic and the Pacific and Sections of the Railway. Second Edition, enlarged. Post 8vo. 10s. 6d.

HISTORY of DISCOVERY in our AUSTRALASIAN COLONIES, Australia, Tasmania, and New Zealand, from the Earliest Date to the Present Day. By WILLIAM HOWITT. 2 vols. 8vo. with 3 Maps, 20s.

The CAPITAL of the TYCOON; a Narrative of a Three Years' Residence in Japan. By Sir RUTHERFORD ALCOCK, K.C.B. 2 vols. 8vo. with numerous Illustrations, 42s.

ZIGZAGGING AMONGST DOLOMITES. By the Author of 'How we Spent the Summer, or a Voyage en Zigzag in Switzerland and Tyrol.' With upwards of 300 Illustrations by the Author. Oblong 4to. price 15s.

The DOLOMITE MOUNTAINS; Excursions through Tyrol, Carinthia, Carniola, and Friuli, 1861-1863. By J. GILBERT and G. C. CHURCHILL, F.R.G.S. With numerous Illustrations. Square crown 8vo. 21s.

GUIDE to the PYRENEES, for the use of Mountaineers. By CHARLES PACKE. 2nd Edition, with Map and Illustrations. Cr. 8vo. 7s. 6d.

The ALPINE GUIDE. By JOHN BALL, M.R.I.A. late President of the Alpine Club. Thoroughly Revised Editions, in Three Volumes, post 8vo. with Maps and other Illustrations:—

GUIDE to the WESTERN ALPS, including Mont Blanc, Monte Rosa, Zermatt, &c. Price 6s. 6d.

GUIDE to the CENTRAL ALPS, including all the Oberland District. Price 7s. 6d.

GUIDE to the EASTERN ALPS, price 10s. 6d.

Introduction on Alpine Travelling in General, and on the Geology of the Alps, price 1s. Each of the Three Volumes or Parts of the *Alpine Guide* may be had with this INTRODUCTION prefixed, price 1s. extra.

The NORTHERN HEIGHTS of LONDON; or, Historical Associations of Hampstead, Highgate, Muswell Hill, Hornsey, and Islington. By WILLIAM HOWITT. With about 40 Woodcuts. Square crown 8vo. 21s.

VISITS to REMARKABLE PLACES: Old Halls, Battle-Fields, and Stones Illustrative of Striking Passages in English History and Poetry. By WILLIAM HOWITT. 2 vols. square crown 8vo. with Woodcuts, 25s.

The **RURAL LIFE of ENGLAND.** By the same Author. With Woodcuts by Bewick and Williams. Medium 8vo. 12s. 6d.

PILGRIMAGES in the PYRENEES and LANDES. By DENYS SHYNE LAWLOR. Crown 8vo. with Frontispiece and Vignette, price 15s.

Works of Fiction.

NOVELS and TALES. By the Right Hon. B. DISRAELI, M.P. Cabinet Edition, complete in Ten Volumes, crown 8vo. price 6s. each, as follows :—

LOTHAIR, 6s.	HENRIETTA TEMPLE, 6s.
CONINGSBY, 6s.	CONTARINI FLEMING, &c. 6s.
SYBIL. 6s.	ALROY, IXION, &c. 6s.
TANCRED, 6s.	The YOUNG DUKE, &c. 6s.
VENETIA, 6s.	VIVIAN GREY, 6s.

The **MODERN NOVELIST'S LIBRARY.** Each Work, in crown 8vo. complete in a Single Volume :—

MELVILLE'S GLADIATORS. 2s. boards; 2s. 6d. cloth.
———— GOOD FOR NOTHING, 2s. boards ; 2s. 6d. cloth.
———— HOLMBY HOUSE. 2s. boards ; 2s. 6d. cloth.
———— INTERPRETER, 2s. boards; 2s. 6d. cloth.
———— KATE COVENTRY, 2s. boards; 2s. 6d. cloth.
———— QUEEN'S MARIES, 2s. boards ; 2s. 6d. cloth.
TROLLOPE'S WARDEN, 1s. 6d. boards; 2s. cloth.
———— BARCHESTER TOWERS. 2s. boards ; 2s. 6d. cloth.
BRAMLEY-MOORE'S SIX SISTERS of the VALLEYS, 2s. boards ; 2s. 6d. cloth.

IERNE; a Tale. By W. STEUART TRENCH, Author of 'Realities of Irish Life.' Second Edition. 2 vols. post 8vo. price 21s.

The **HOME at HEATHERBRAE; a Tale.** By the Author of 'Everley.' Fcp. 8vo. price 5s.

CABINET EDITION of STORIES and TALES by Miss SEWELL:—

AMY HERBERT, 2s. 6d.	IVORS, 3s. 6d.
GERTRUDE, 2s. 6d.	KATHARINE ASHTON, 3s. 6d.
The EARL'S DAUGHTER. 2s. 6d.	MARGARET PERCIVAL, 5s.
EXPERIENCE of LIFE, 2s. 6d.	LANETON PARSONAGE, 4s. 6d.
CLEVE HALL, 3s. 6d.	URSULA, 4s. 6d.

STORIES and TALES. By E. M. SEWELL. Comprising:—Amy Herbert; Gertrude; The Earl's Daughter; The Experience of Life; Cleve Hall; Ivors; Katharine Ashton; Margaret Percival; Laneton Parsonage; and Ursula. The Ten Works, complete in Eight Volumes, crown 8vo. bound in leather, and contained in a Box, price 42s.

A Glimpse of the World. By the Author of 'Amy Herbert.' Fcp. 7s. 6d.

The Journal of a Home Life. By the same Author. Post 8vo. 9s. 6d.

After Life ; a Sequel to ' The Journal of a Home Life.' Price 10s. 6d.

UNCLE PETER'S FAIRY TALE for the NINETEENTH CENTURY. Edited by E. M. SEWELL, Author of 'Amy Herbert,' &c. Fcp. 8vo. 7s. 6d.

THE GIANT; A Witch's Story for English Boys. By the same Author and Editor. Fcp. 8vo. price 5s.

WONDERFUL STORIES from NORWAY, SWEDEN, and ICELAND. Adapted and arranged by JULIA GODDARD. With an Introductory Essay by the Rev. G. W. COX, M.A. and Six Woodcuts. Square post 8vo. 6s.

A VISIT to MY DISCONTENTED COUSIN. Reprinted, with some Additions, from *Fraser's Magazine*. Crown 8vo. price 7s. 6d.

BECKER'S GALLUS; or, Roman Scenes of the Time of Augustus: with Notes and Excursuses. New Edition. Post 8vo. 7s. 6d.

BECKER'S CHARICLES; a Tale illustrative of Private Life among the Ancient Greeks: with Notes and Excursuses. New Edition. Post 8vo. 7s. 6d.

CABINET EDITION of NOVELS and TALES by G. J. WHYTE MELVILLE:—

The GLADIATORS. 7s.	HOLMBY HOUSE, 5s.
DIGBY GRAND. 5s.	GOOD *for* NOTHING, 6s.
KATE COVENTRY. 5s.	*The* QUEEN's MARIES, 6s.
GENERAL BOUNCE, 5s.	*The* INTERPRETER, 5s.

TALES of ANCIENT GREECE. By GEORGE W. COX, M.A. late Scholar of Trin. Coll. Oxon. Crown 8vo. price 6s. 6d.

A MANUAL of MYTHOLOGY, in the form of Question and Answer. By the same Author. Fcp. 3s.

OUR CHILDREN'S STORY, by one of their Gossips. By the Author of 'Voyage en Zigzag,' 'Pictures in Tyrol,' &c. Small 4to. with Sixty Illustrations by the Author, price 10s. 6d.

Poetry and The Drama.

THOMAS MOORE'S POETICAL WORKS, the only Editions containing the Author's last Copyright Additions:—
CABINET EDITION, 10 vols. fcp. 8vo. price 35s.
SHAMROCK EDITION, crown 8vo. price 3s. 6d.
RUBY EDITION. crown 8vo. with Portrait, price 6s.
LIBRARY EDITION, medium 8vo. Portrait and Vignette, 14s.
PEOPLE's EDITION, square crown 8vo. with Portrait, &c. 10s. 6d.

MOORE'S IRISH MELODIES, Maclise's Edition, with 161 Steel Plates from Original Drawings. Super-royal 8vo. 31s. 6d.

Miniature Edition of Moore's Irish Melodies with Maclise's Designs (as above) reduced in Lithography. Imp. 16mo. 10s. 6d.

MOORE'S LALLA ROOKH. Tenniel's Edition, with 68 Wood Engravings from original Drawings and other Illustrations. Fcp. 4to. 21s.

SOUTHEY'S POETICAL WORKS, with the Author's last Corrections and copyright Additions. Library Edition, in 1 vol. medium 8vo. with Portrait and Vignette, 14s.

LAYS of ANCIENT ROME; with *Ivry* and the *Armada*. By the Right Hon. LORD MACAULAY. 16mo. 4s. 6d.

Lord Macaulay's Lays of Ancient Rome. With 90 Illustrations on Wood, from the Antique, from Drawings by G. SCHARF. Fcp. 4to. 21s.

Miniature Edition of Lord Macaulay's Lays of Ancient Rome, with the Illustrations (as above) reduced in Lithography. Imp. 16mo. 10s. 6d.

GOLDSMITH'S POETICAL WORKS, with Wood Engravings from Designs by Members of the ETCHING CLUB. Imperial 16mo. 7s. 6d.

JOHN JERNINGHAM'S JOURNAL. Fcp. 8vo. price 3s. 6d.

POEMS OF BYGONE YEARS. Edited by the Author of 'Amy Herbert,' &c. Fcp. 8vo. price 5s.

POEMS. By JEAN INGELOW. Fifteenth Edition. Fcp. 8vo. 5s.

EUCHARIS; a Poem. By F. RÉGINALD STATHAM (Francis Reynolds), Author of 'Alice Rushton, and other Poems' and 'Glaphyra, and other Poems.' Fcp. 8vo. price 3s. 6d.

POEMS by Jean Ingelow. With nearly 100 Illustrations by Eminent Artists, engraved on Wood by the Brothers DALZIEL. Fcp. 4to. 21s.

The **MAD WAR PLANET,** and other **POEMS.** By WILLIAM HOWITT, Author of 'Visits to Remarkable Places,' &c. Fcp. 8vo. price 5s.

MOPSA the FAIRY. By JEAN INGELOW. Pp. 256, with Eight Illustrations engraved on Wood. Fcp. 8vo. 6s.

A STORY of DOOM, and other Poems. By JEAN INGELOW. Third Edition. Fcp. 5s.

WORKS by EDWARD YARDLEY:—
> FANTASTIC STORIES. Fcp. 3s. 6d.
> MELUSINE and OTHER POEMS. Fcp. 5s.
> HORACE'S ODES, *translated into* English Verse. Crown 8vo. 6s.
> SUPPLEMENTARY STORIES and POEMS. Fcp. 3s. 6d.

BOWDLER'S FAMILY SHAKSPEARE, cheaper Genuine Editions. Medium 8vo. large type, with 36 WOODCUTS, price 14s. Cabinet Edition, with the same ILLUSTRATIONS, 6 vols. fcp. 3s. 6d. each.

HORATII OPERA, Pocket Edition, with carefully corrected Text, Marginal References, and Introduction. Edited by the Rev. J. E. YONGE, M.A. Square 18mo. 4s. 6d.

HORATII OPERA. Library Edition, with Marginal References and English Notes. Edited by the Rev. J. E. YONGE. 8vo. 21s.

The **ÆNEID of VIRGIL** Translated into English Verse. By JOHN CONINGTON, M.A. New Edition. Crown 8vo. 9s.

ARUNDINES CAMI, sive Musarum Cantabrigiensium Lusus canori. Collegit atque edidit H. DRURY, M.A. Editio Sexta, curavit H. J. HODGSON, M.A. Crown 8vo. 7s. 6d.

HUNTING SONGS and **MISCELLANEOUS VERSES.** By R. E. EGERTON WARBURTON. Second Edition. Fcp. 8vo. 5s.

— — — — — —

Rural Sports, &c.

ENCYCLOPÆDIA of RURAL SPORTS; a complete Account, Historical, Practical, and Descriptive, of Hunting, Shooting, Fishing, Racing, and all other Rural and Athletic Sports and Pastimes. By D. P. BLAINE. With above 600 Woodcuts (20 from Designs by JOHN LEECH). 8vo. 21s.

The **DEAD SHOT**, or Sportsman's Complete Guide ; a Treatise on the Use of the Gun, Dog-breaking, Pigeon-shooting, &c. By MARKSMAN. Revised Edition. Fcp. 8vo. with Plates, 5s.

The **FLY-FISHER'S ENTOMOLOGY**. By ALFRED RONALDS. With coloured Representations of the Natural and Artificial Insect. Sixth Edition ; with 20 coloured Plates. 8vo. 14s.

A **BOOK** on **ANGLING** ; a complete Treatise on the Art of Angling in every branch. By FRANCIS FRANCIS. Second Edition, with Portrait and 15 other Plates, plain and coloured. Post 8vo. 15s.

The **BOOK of the ROACH**. By GREVILLE FENNELL, of ' The Field.' Fcp. 8vo. price 2s. 6d.

WILCOCKS'S SEA-FISHERMAN ; comprising the Chief Methods of Hook and Line Fishing in the British and other Seas, a Glance at Nets, and Remarks on Boats and Boating. Second Edition, enlarged ; with 80 Woodcuts. Post 8vo. 12s. 6d.

HORSES and STABLES. By Colonel F. FITZWYGRAM, XV. the King's Hussars. With Twenty-four Plates of Illustrations, containing very numerous Figures engraved on Wood. 8vo. 15s.

The **HORSE'S FOOT**, and **HOW to KEEP IT SOUND**. By W. MILES, Esq. Ninth Edition, with Illustrations. Imperial 8vo. 12s. 6d.

A **PLAIN TREATISE** on **HORSE-SHOEING**. By the same Author. Sixth Edition. Post 8vo. with Illustrations, 2s. 6d.

STABLES and STABLE-FITTINGS. By the same. Imp. 8vo. with 13 Plates, 15s.

REMARKS on **HORSES' TEETH**, addressed to Purchasers. By the same. Post 8vo. 1s. 6d.

ROBBINS'S CAVALRY CATECHISM, or Instructions on Cavalry Exercise and Field Movements, Brigade Movements, Out-post Duty, Cavalry supporting Artillery, Artillery attached to Cavalry. 12mo. 5s.

BLAINE'S VETERINARY ART ; a Treatise on the Anatomy, Physiology, and Curative Treatment of the Diseases of the Horse, Neat Cattle and Sheep. Seventh Edition, revised and enlarged by C. STEEL, M.R.C.V.S.L. 8vo. with Plates and Woodcuts, 18s.

The **HORSE** ; with a Treatise on Draught. By WILLIAM YOUATT. New Edition, revised and enlarged. 8vo. with numerous Woodcuts, 12s. 6d.

The **DOG**. By the same Author. 8vo. with numerous Woodcuts, 6s.

The **DOG in HEALTH and DISEASE**. By STONEHENGE. With 70 Wood Engravings. Square crown 8vo. 10s. 6d.

The **GREYHOUND**. By STONEHENGE. Revised Edition, with 24 Portraits of Greyhounds. Square crown 8vo. 10s. 6d.

The **OX** ; his Diseases and their Treatment: with an Essay on Parturition in the Cow. By J. R. DOBSON. Crown 8vo. with Illustrations. 7s. 6d.

Works of *Utility* and *General Information.*

The **THEORY** and **PRACTICE** of **BANKING**. By H. D. MACLEOD, M.A. Barrister-at-Law. Second Edition, entirely remodelled. 2 vols. 8vo. 30s.

A DICTIONARY, Practical, Theoretical, and Historical, of Commerce and Commercial Navigation. By J. R. M'CULLOCH. New and thoroughly revised Edition. 8vo. price 63s. cloth, or 70s. half-bd. in russia.

The LAW of NATIONS Considered as Independent Political Communities. By Sir TRAVERS TWISS, D.C.L. 2 vols. 8vo. 30s.; or separately, PART I. *Peace*, 12s. PART II. *War*, 18s.

The CABINET LAWYER; a Popular Digest of the Laws of England, Civil, Criminal, and Constitutional: intended for Practical Use and General Information. Twenty-third Edition. Fcp. 8vo. price 7s. 6d.

PEWTNER'S COMPREHENSIVE SPECIFIER; A Guide to the Practical Specification of every kind of Building-Artificers' Work; with Forms of Building Conditions and Agreements, an Appendix, Foot-Notes, and a copious Index. Edited by W. YOUNG, Architect. Crown 8vo. price 6s.

The LAW RELATING to BENEFIT BUILDING SOCIETIES; with Practical Observations on the Act and all the Cases decided thereon; also a Form of Rules and Forms of Mortgages. By W. TIDD PRATT, Barrister. Second Edition. Fcp. 3s. 6d.

COLLIERIES and COLLIERS: a Handbook of the Law and Leading Cases relating thereto. By J. C. FOWLER, of the Inner Temple, Barrister. Second Edition. Fcp. 8vo. 7s. 6d.

The MATERNAL MANAGEMENT of CHILDREN in HEALTH and Disease. By THOMAS BULL, M.D. Fcp. 5s.

HINTS to MOTHERS on the MANAGEMENT of their HEALTH during the Period of Pregnancy and in the Lying-in Room. By the late THOMAS BULL, M.D. Fcp. 5s.

HOW to NURSE SICK CHILDREN; containing Directions which may be found of service to all who have charge of the Young. By CHARLES WEST, M.D. Second Edition. Fcp. 8vo. 1s. 6d.

NOTES on LYING-IN INSTITUTIONS; with a Proposal for Organising an Institution for Training Midwives and Midwifery Nurses. By FLORENCE NIGHTINGALE. With several Illustrations. 8vo. price 7s. 6d.

NOTES on HOSPITALS. By FLORENCE NIGHTINGALE. Third Edition, enlarged; with 13 Plans. Post 4to. 18s.

CHESS OPENINGS. By F. W. LONGMAN, Balliol College, Oxford. Fcp. 8vo. 2s. 6d.

A PRACTICAL TREATISE on BREWING; with Formulæ for Public Brewers, and Instructions for Private Families. By W. BLACK. 8vo. 10s. 6d.

MODERN COOKERY for PRIVATE FAMILIES, reduced to a System of Easy Practice in a Series of carefully-tested Receipts. By ELIZA ACTON. Newly revised and enlarged Edition; with 8 Plates of Figures and 150 Woodcuts. Fcp. 6s.

WILLICH'S POPULAR TABLES, for ascertaining, according to the Carlisle Table of Mortality, the value of Lifehold, Leasehold, and Church Property, Renewal Fines, Reversions, &c. Seventh Edition, edited by MONTAGUE MARRIOTT, Barrister-at-Law. Post 8vo. price 10s.

MAUNDER'S TREASURY of KNOWLEDGE and LIBRARY of Reference: comprising an English Dictionary and Grammar, Universal Gazetteer, Classical Dictionary, Chronology, Law Dictionary, a Synopsis of the Peerage, useful Tables, &c. Revised Edition. Fcp. 8vo. price 6s.

INDEX.

ACTON'S Modern Cookery 28
ALCOCK'S Residence in Japan 23
ALLEN'S Four Discourses of Chrysostom .. 22
ALLIES on Formation of Christendom 21
Alpine Guide (The) 23
ALTHAUS on Medical Electricity 14
ARNOLD'S Manual of English Literature .. 7
ARNOTT'S Elements of Physics 11
Arundines Cami 26
Autumn Holidays of a Country Parson 8
AYRE'S Treasury of Bible Knowledge...... 20

BACON'S Essays, by WHATELY 6
———— Life and Letters, by SPEDDING .. 5
———— Works, edited by SPEDDING 6
BAIN'S Logic, Deductive and Inductive 10
———— Mental and Moral Science 10
———— on the Senses and Intellect........... 10
BALL'S Alpine Guide 23
BAYLDON'S Rents and Tillages 19
Beaten Tracks 23
BECKER'S Charicles and Gallus 25
BENFEY'S Sanskrit Dictionary 8
BERNARD on British Neutrality............ 1
BLACK'S Treatise on Brewing 24
BLACKLEY'S German-English Dictionary... 8
BLAINE'S Rural Sports 26
———— Veterinary Art 27
BOOTH'S Saint-Simon 3
BOULTBEE on 39 Articles 19
BOURNE on Screw Propeller 18
BOURNE'S Catechism of the Steam Engine . 18
————Handbook of the Steam Engine 19
————Improvements in the Steam Engine ....
————Treatise on the Steam Engine .. 18
————Examples of Modern Engines .. 18
BOWDLER'S Family SHAKSPEARE 26
BOYD'S Reminiscences 1
BRAMLEY-MOORE'S Six Sisters of the Valleys................................ 24
BRANDE'S Dictionary of Science, Literature, and Art....................... 13
BRAY'S (C.) Education of the Feelings 10
———— Philosophy of Necessity........ 10
———— on Force...................... 10
BROWNE'S Exposition of the 39 Articles.... 19
BRUNEL'S Life of BRUNEL 4
BUCKLE'S History of Civilization 3
BULL'S Hints to Mothers 28
———— Maternal Management of Children 24
BUNSEN'S God in History 3
———— Prayers 19
BURKE'S Vicissitudes of Families.......... 5
BURTON'S Christian Church.............. 4

Cabinet Lawyer 28
CAMPBELL'S Norway 22

CARNOTA'S Memoirs of Pombal 4
CATES'S Biographical Dictionary 5
CATS' and FARLIE'S Moral Emblems 16
Changed Aspects of Unchanged Truths 9
CHESNEY'S Indian Polity 3
———— Waterloo Campaign............ 2
———— and REEVE'S Military Essays .. 2
Chorale Book for England................. 16
CLOUGH'S Lives from Plutarch 2
COLENSO (Bishop) on Pentateuch 21
Commonplace Philosopher 8
CONINGTON'S Translation of the Æneid.... 26
CONTANSEAU'S French-English Dictionaries 8
CONYBEARE and HOWSON'S St. Paul 20
COTTON'S (Bishop) Life 5
COOPER'S Surgical Dictionary............. 15
COPLAND'S Dictionary of Practical Medicine 15
Counsel and Comfort from a City Pulpit.... 9
COX'S Aryan Mythology.................... 3
———— Manual of Mythology 25
———— Tale of the Great Persian War 2
———— Tales of Ancient Greece......... 25
CRESY'S Encyclopædia of Civil Engineering 14
Critical Essays of a Country Parson 8
CROOKES on Beet-Root Sugar 15
———'s Chemical Analysis 14
CULLEY'S Handbook of Telegraphy........ 18
CUSACK'S History of Ireland.............. 3

D'AUBIGNE'S History of the Reformation in the time of CALVIN 2
DAVIDSON'S Introduction to New Testament 20
Dead Shot (The), by MARKSMAN 27
DE LA RIVE'S Treatise on Electricity 12
DENISON'S Vice-Regal Life 1
DE TOCQUEVILLE'S Democracy in America 2
DISRAELI'S Lothair 24
———— Novels and Tales 24
DORELL'S Medical Reports 15
DOBSON on the Ox 27
DOVE on Storms 11
DOYLE'S Fairyland 16
DYER'S City of Rome 2

EASTLAKE'S Hints on Household Taste 17
———— History of Oil Painting 17
————Gothic Revival............... 17
————Life of Gibson 16
Elements of Botany 13
ELLICOTT on the Revision of the English New Testament............... 19
———— Commentary on Ephesians 20
———— Commentary on Galatians 20
———— Pastoral Epist. 20
———— Philippians, &c. 20
———— Thessalonians 20
———— Lectures on the Life of Christ.. 20

Essays and Contributions of A. K. H. B..... 8
EWALD's History of Israel.................. 20

FAIRBAIRN on Iron Shipbuilding.......... 18
————'s Applications of Iron.......... 18
———— Information for Engineers .. 18
———— Mills and Millwork 18
FARADAY's Life and Letters.................. 4
FARRAR's Families of Speech 9
————Chapters on Language 7
FELKIN on Hosiery and Lace Manufactures 18
FENNELL'S Book of the Roach.............. 27
FFOULKES'S Christendom's Divisions 21
FITZWYGRAM on Horses and Stables 27
FOWLER's Collieries and Colliers 28
FRANCIS's Fishing Book.................... 27
FRESHFIELD's Travels in the Caucasus.... 23
FROUDE's History of England............... 1
————Short Studies on Great Subjects 9

GANOT's Elementary Physics 11
GILBERT's Cadore, or Titian's Country 22
GILBERT and CHURCHILL's Dolomites 23
GIRDLESTONE'S Bible Synonymes 19
GLEDSTONE'S Life of WHITEFIELD 5
GODDARD's Wonderful Stories 25
GOLDSMITH's Poems, Illustrated 26
GRAHAM's View of Literature and Art 3
GRANT's Home Politics 6
———— Ethics of Aristotle................ 6
Graver Thoughts of a Country Parson..... 8
GRAY'S Anatomy 15
GREENHOW on Bronchitis 15
GRIFFITH's Fundamentals 19
GROVE on Correlation of Physical Forces .. 12
GURNEY's Chapters of French History 2
GWILT'S Encyclopædia of Architecture 17

HAMPDEN's (Bishop) Memorials 4
HARE on Election of Representatives 7
HARTWIG's Harmonies of Nature 13
———— Polar World................... 13
———— Sea and its Living Wonders .. 13
———— Subterranean World 13
———— Tropical World 13
HAUGHTON's Manual of Geology 12
HERSCHEL's Outlines of Astronomy........ 10
HEWITT on Diseases of Women 14
HODGSON's Theory of Practice 10
———— Time and Space 10
HOLMES's System of Surgery 14
————Surgical Diseases of Infancy.... 14
Home (The) at Heatherbrae............... 24
HORNE's Introduction to the Scriptures.... 20
———— Compendium of ditto 20
How we Spent the Summer 23
HOWITT's Australian Discovery............ 23
————Mad War Planet................ 26
————Northern Heights of London.... 23
————Rural Life of England.......... 24
————Visits to Remarkable Places.... 24

HÜBNER's Memoir of Sixtus V............. 2
HUGHES's (W.) Manual of Geography 11
HUME'S Essays 10
————Treatise on Human Nature 10

IHNE's Roman History 2
INGELOW's Poems 26
———— Story of Doom 26
———— Mopsa 26

JAMESON's Saints and Martyrs 17
———— Legends of the Madonna........ 17
———— Monastic Orders 17
JAMESON and EASTLAKE's Saviour 17
John Jerningham's Journal 26
JOHNSTON's Geographical Dictionary...... 11

KALISCH's Commentary on the Bible 7
———— Hebrew Grammar 7
KEITH on Fulfilment of Prophecy.......... 20
———— Destiny of the World 20
KERL's Metallurgy 18
RÖHRIG 18
KIRBY and SPENCE'S Entomology.......... 13

LATHAM's English Dictionary.............. 7
LAWLOR's Pilgrimages in the Pyrenees 24
LECKY's History of European Morals 3
———— Rationalism 3
Leisure Hours in Town 9
Lessons of Middle Age 9
LEWES' History of Philosophy 3
LIDDELL and SCOTT's Two Lexicons 8
Life of Man Symbolised 16
LINDLEY and MOORE's Treasury of Botany 13
LONGMAN's Edward the Third 2
———— Lectures on the History of Eng-
land 2
———— Chess Openings 28
LOUDON's Agriculture 19
———— Gardening 19
———— Plants 13
LOWNDES's Engineer's Handbook 17
LUBBOCK on Origin of Civilisation.......... 12
Lyra Eucharistica 22
————Germanica 16, 21
————Messianica 22
————Mystica........................ 22

MACAULAY's (Lord) Essays 3
————History of England .. 1
————Lays of Ancient Rome 25
————Miscellaneous Writings 9
————Speeches 7
————Complete Works...... 1
MACFARREN's Lectures on Harmony 16
MACLEOD'S Elements of Political Economy 7
———— Dictionary of Political Eco-
nomy 7
———— Theory and Practice of Banking 27
McCULLOCH's Dictionary of Commerce.... 28

MAGUIRE'S Life of Father Mathew 5
——— Pope Pius IX.................... 5
MALET'S Overthrow of the Germanic Con-
federation by Prussia..................... 2
MANNING'S England and Christendom 21
MARCET on the Larynx 15
MARSHALL'S Canadian Dominion.......... 11
——— Physiology.................... 15
MARSHMAN'S Life of Havelock 5
——— History of India 3
MARTINEAU'S Christian Life 22
MASSINGBERD'S History of the Reformation 4
MAUNDER'S Biographical Treasury........ 5
——— Geographical Treasury 11
——— Historical Treasury 4
——— Scientific and Literary Trea-
sury.......................... 13
——— Treasury of Knowledge...... 28
——— Treasury of Natural History 13
MAY's Constitutional History of England.. 1
MELVILLE'S Novels and Tales .... 24 & 25
MENDELSSOHN'S Letters 5
MERIVALE'S Fall of the Roman Republic.. 3
——— Romans under the Empire 3
MERRIFIELD and EVER'S Navigation 11
MILES on Horse's Foot and Horseshoeing .. 27
——— Horses' Teeth and Stables 27
MILL (J.) on the Mind 9
MILL (J. S.) on Liberty 6
——— on Representative Government 6
——— on Utilitarianism............. 6
MILL'S (J. S.) Dissertations and Discussions 6
——— Political Economy 6
——— System of Logic............. 6
——— Hamilton's Philosophy...... 6
——— Inaugural Address 7
——— Subjection of Women........ 6
MILLER'S Elements of Chemistry 14
——— Hymn-Writers 21
MITCHELL'S Manual of Architecture 17
——— Manual of Assaying 18
MONSELL'S Beatitudes..................... 22
——— His Presence not his Memory 22
——— 'Spiritual Songs'............. 22
MOORE'S Irish Melodies 25
——— Lalla Rookh 25
——— Poetical Works 25
MORELL'S Elements of Psychology 9
——— Mental Philosophy............. 9
MULLER'S (MAX) Chips from a German
Workshop 9
——— Lectures on Language 7
——— (K. O.) Literature of Ancient
Greece 2
MURCHISON on Liver Complaints.......... 15
MURE'S Language and Literature of Greece 2

NASH'S Compendium of the Prayer Book.. 19
New Testament, Illustrated Edition........ 16
NEWMAN'S History of his Religious Opinions 5
NIGHTINGALE'S Notes on Hospitals 24
——— Lying-In Insti-
tutions.................... 24
NILSSON'S Scandinavia 12

NORTHCOTT'S Lathes and Turning 17

ODLING'S Animal Chemistry 14
——— Course of Practical Chemistry.. 14
——— Manual of Chemistry............. 14
——— Lectures on Carbon 14
——— Outlines of Chemistry............. 14
O'DRISCOLL'S Memoirs of MACLISE........ 4
O'FLANAGAN'S Irish Chancellors 5
Our Children's Story........................ 25
OWEN'S Lectures on the Invertebrate...... 12
——— Comparative Anatomy and Physio-
logy of Vertebrate Animals 12

PACKE'S Guide to the Pyrenees 23
PAGET'S Lectures on Surgical Pathology .. 15
PEREIRA'S Manual of Materia Medica 16
PERKIN'S Italian and Tuscan Sculptors.... 17
PERRING'S Churches and Creeds 19
PEWTNER'S Comprehensive Specifier 28
Pictures in Tyrol........................... 23
PIESSE'S Art of Perfumery 19
——— Natural Magic.................. 19
PONTON'S Beginning....................... 12
PRATT'S Law of Building Societies 24
PRENDERGAST'S Mastery of Languages.... 8
PRESCOTT'S Scripture Difficulties 21
Present-Day Thoughts...................... 9
PROCTOR on Plurality of Worlds 10
——— Saturn and its System........ 10
——— The Sun 10
——— 's Scientific Essays 12
Public Schools Atlas (The) 11

RAE'S Westward by Rail.................... 23
Recreations of a Country Parson............ 8
REICHEL'S See of Rome 20
REILLY'S Map of Mont Blanc 23
REIMANN on Aniline Dyes.................. 15
RIVERS' Rose Amateur's Guide 13
ROBBINS'S Cavalry Catechism.............. 27
ROGERS'S Correspondence of Greyson...... 9
——— Eclipse of Faith 9
——— Defence of ditto.................. 9
ROGET'S English Words and Phrases....... 7
RONALD'S Fly-Fisher's Entomology 27
ROSE'S Ignatius Loyola 2
ROTHSCHILD'S Israelites.................... 20
ROWTON'S Debater 7
RUSSELL'S Pau and the Pyrenees.......... 22

SANDARS'S Justinian's Institutes 5
SAVILE on the Truth of the Bible 19
SCHALLEN'S Spectrum Analysis............. 11
SCOTT'S Lectures on the Fine Arts 16
——— Albert Durer 16
SEEBOHM'S Oxford Reformers of 1498...... 2
SEWELL'S After Life....................... 24
——— Amy Herbert 24
——— Cleve Hall...................... 24
——— Earl's Daughter................. 24
——— Examination for Confirmation .. 21

SEWELL'S Experience of Life 24
———— Gertrude....................... 24
———— Giant 25
———— Glimpse of the World 24
———— History of the Early Church 2
———— Ivors..................... 24
———— Journal of a Home Life.......... 24
———— Katharine Ashton................ 24
———— Laneton Parsonage 24
———— Margaret Percival 24
———— Passing Thoughts on Religion .. 21
———— Poems of Bygone Years 26
———— Preparations for Communion.... 21
———— Principles of Education.......... 21
———— Readings for Confirmation 21
———— Readings for Lent................ 21
———— Tales and Stories 21
———— Thoughts for the Age............. 21
———— Ursula........................... 21
———— Thoughts for the Holy Week.... 21
SHIPLEY'S Four Cardinal Virtues.......... 21
———— Invocation of Saints 22
SHORT'S Church History..................... 4
SMART'S WALKER'S Dictionary 8
SMITH'S (V.) Bible and Popular Theology 19
———— (J.) Paul's Voyage and Shipwreck 20
———— (SYDNEY) Miscellaneous Works.. 9
———— ———— Wit and Wisdom 9
———— ———— Life and Letters........ 4
SOUTHEY'S Doctor 7
———— Poetical Works 25
STANLEY'S History of British Birds 13
STATHAM'S Eucharis 26
STEBBING'S Analysis of MILL'S Logic 6
STEPHEN'S Ecclesiastical Biography 5
———— Playground of Europe.......... 22
STIRLING'S Secret of Hegel 9
———— Sir WILLIAM HAMILTON 10
STONEHENGE on the Dog 27
———— on the Greyhound............ 27
STRICKLAND'S Queens of England.......... 5
Sunday Afternoons at the Parish Church of
   a Scottish University City (St. Andrews).. 8

TAYLOR'S History of India 3
———— (Jeremy) Works, edited by EDEN 22
THIRLWALL'S History of Greece........... 2
THOMPSON S (Archbishop) Laws of Thought 6
———— —(A. T.) Conspectus 16
TODD (A.) on Parliamentary Government 1
TODD and BOWMAN'S Anatomy and Phy-
   siology of Man...................... 15
TRENCH'S Ierne, a Tale 24
TRENCH'S Realities of Irish Life 3
TROLLOPE'S Barchester Towers 24
———— Warden 24
TWISS'S Law of Nations.................... 26
TYNDALL on Diamagnetism................ 11
——— ——— Electricity.................. 12

TYNDALL on Heat........................ 11
——— ——— Imagination in Science 12
——— ——— Sound 11
——— ——— 's Faraday as a Discoverer...... 4
——— ——— Fragments of Science.......... 12
——— ——— Hours of Exercise in the Alps.. 22
——— ——— Lectures on Light.............. 12

UEBERWEG'S System of Logic 9
UNCLE PETER'S Fairy Tale 24
URE'S Arts, Manufactures, and Mines...... 17

VAN DER HOEVEN'S Handbook of Zoology 18
VEREKER'S Sunny South 22
Visit to my Discontented Cousin 25

WARBURTON'S Hunting Songs 26
WATSON'S Principles and Practice of Physic 14
WATTS'S Dictionary of Chemistry 14
WEBB'S Objects for Common Telescopes .. 11
WEBSTER and WILKINSON'S Greek Testa-
   ment 21
WELLINGTON'S Life, by GLEIG 5
WEST on Children's Diseases................ 14
———— Nursing Sick Children............ 28
———— 's Lumleian Lectures 14
WHATELY'S English Synonymes 6
———— Logic 6
———— Rhetoric 6
WHATELY on a Future State 21
———— Truth of Christianity 2
WHITE'S Latin-English Dictionaries 7
WILCOCK'S Sea Fisherman................. 27
WILLIAMS'S Aristotle's Ethics 6
WILLIAMS on Climate of South of France 15
———— ———Consumption 15
WILLICH'S Popular Tables 28
WILLIS'S Principles of Mechanism 17
WINSLOW on Light 12
WOOD'S Bible Animals 12
———— Homes without Hands 13
———— Insects at Home 13
———— Strange Dwellings 13
WOODWARD and CATES'S Encyclopædia.. 4

YARDLEY'S Poetical Works................. 26
YONGE'S English-Greek Lexicons.......... 8
———— Two Editions of Horace 26
———— History of England 1
YOUATT on the Dog 27
———— on the Horse 27

ZELLER'S Socrates 6
———— Stoics, Epicureans, and Sceptics.. 6
Zigzagging amongst Dolomites 23

Spottiswoode & Co., Printers, New-street Square, London.

www.ingramcontent.com/pod-product-compliance
Lightning Source LLC
Chambersburg PA
CBHW020102030726
47498CB00006B/1913

* 9 7 8 3 3 3 7 0 8 2 3 3 8 *